Trouble with the Exe

Lockwood and Darrow Mysteries
Book 3

Suzy Bussell

Sigbit Press

Trouble with the Exe

By

Suzy Bussell

Chapter One

A ngus Darrow stopped the engine of his black VW Golf and got out.

He'd parked on a driveway in Topsham, just outside Exeter, next to a plush dark blue Bentley, the owner of which lived inside the house in front of him.

The house was the most exclusive in the town, with a commanding view of the River Exe. Dressed in a smart dark blue pinstripe suit, white shirt and blue tie, he admired the view for a moment, then walked to the front door to find the owner: his work partner, Charlotte Lockwood.

Grigore, Charlotte's driver, let him in, and he found her in her study, a large, elegantly decorated room on the ground floor with a cream carpet and a large oak desk.

Charlotte and Angus were private investigators and had been working together for months now, after Charlotte, a computer expert, had insisted she help him. Most days, Angus came over to her house to work. Today they planned to talk about which case they would look at next.

Charlotte was tapping at the keyboard of her computer. "Good morning," she said brightly and looked up when he entered, not pausing her typing. Her blonde hair was in a ponytail, and she was wearing a chic navy shift dress.

"Hacking into the Pentagon again?" Angus pulled a chair out and sat down, a small smile on his lips.

"Of course. I do it every day. It's amazing what you can find out. Area 52, CIA double agents, FBI conspiracies…"

Angus chuckled.

"You've come to talk about our next case. Have there been many enquiries lately?" She paused a moment, then started typing again, looking at the screen.

"I've taken on a background check," Angus said in a flat tone.

"No more cheating spouses to follow?"

"There are always plenty of those."

It was true. Cheating spouses, or rather partners, made up 90 percent of enquiries. If there was a lull in work, Angus would take one on. But most of the time it was just paranoid partners with trust issues. He was also careful to only take on those cases when he was sure his client wasn't doing it because of coercive control. When he'd been a police detective, he'd come across too many people like that. Jealous lovers, who were controlling their partner's life in every way. He wondered why, with the technology available now to track people, so many people still wanted this type of service.

"Are you bored of checking that people aren't cheating?" Charlotte grinned. "Or rather, *are* cheating, because so far, all the ones we've looked into have been. It's enough to put you off a relationship for life."

"No, but I've prioritised this one."

That made her stop typing and look at him. "Are you going to tell me why?"

"It's a favour for an old friend."

"A freebie? That's unlike you."

"I'm not doing it for free. I'm putting it at the top of the list."

Charlotte considered. "I wonder what sort of person you would put at the top of your list? It's not as though you're normally secretive about anything." She was being sarcastic. Angus rarely volunteered information about his private life, and he knew she found it extremely irritating. Which made him do it all the more.

Charlotte was much more open about everything, and her therapist, Misty, was always telling her to rein in her blathering about her every thought and feeling to her friends. But she couldn't help it, and now that she was approaching fifty, she didn't care any more either.

She reached for the pad and pen at the side of the desk and handed them to him. "Write down their name and everything you know about them, and I'll start an in-depth internet search."

Angus wrote, then turned the pad round to Charlotte.

She looked at it. "All right, let's see what we can find out about ... Mr Nigel Starling."

She opened a browser and started to type. The doorbell sounded, but Charlotte didn't move. Instead, her driver and hired muscle, Grigore, shouted from the hallway, "I go," in his thick Romanian accent.

There was a distant sound of the door opening and some mumbled talk, then from the doorway, "Hello, Charlotte."

Charlotte looked up instantly. A woman in her mid-forties, with a centimetre of dark roots showing in her blonde hair, stood in the doorway. She was dressed in blue leggings and an oversized white shirt, with a pained expression on her face.

There was a long pause. Too long.

Charlotte stood up. "What the hell are you doing in my house?" she said in a carefully controlled tone.

"That's not very nice." The woman put her hand on her hip, just like Charlotte did when she was fighting to contain her emotions.

"Not nice? Not nice, she says." Charlotte looked at Angus, then thrust a hand towards the woman. "This is Michelle. My former best friend, right up to the moment she stole my husband after starting a torrid affair with him. And she says *I'm* not nice." She moved around the desk. "Get out of my house." Her tone was firm, but there was menace in it.

Both women stared at each other, not moving. Angus wondered whether he would have to stop them fighting, in a moment.

"Fine." Charlotte walked to her desk and pressed a button underneath it.

A moment later, Grigore appeared behind Michelle.

"Grigore, remove this woman from my house," Charlotte said tersely.

He nodded and stepped forward.

The woman turned and looked at him, then folded her arms in defiance.

"Now, please," Charlotte said.

Grigore put his arms around Michelle and easily lifted her up. Her legs splayed in different directions and she tried to stop him by trying to shake free. "Stop! Listen to me, Charlotte. I need your help. Listen..."

"I wouldn't listen to you if you were the last person on earth!" Charlotte shouted.

"*Please...*" they heard from the hallway, just before the front door slammed.

Charlotte sat down at her desk and buried her head in her hands. "Calm, happy place," she muttered. "Misty. I need to call Misty."

There was a long silence. No sound came from outside or from the hallway, although they were too far away from the front of the house to hear much.

Angus sat looking at Charlotte, genuinely lost for words.

The sound of the front door slamming again filled the house. Grigore appeared. "She no go. She difficult woman. She say she need talk to you," he said, his Romanian accent even stronger than usual.

Charlotte lifted her head. "Has she parked in the drive?"

He nodded.

She got up. "My therapist will hate me for what I'm about to do. But that's nothing compared to how much I'll hate myself..."

Angus's eyes narrowed. "What are you going to do?"

"I'm going to get into my Bentley and push her car onto the road."

Angus frowned. "Won't that damage it?"

Charlotte shrugged. "I'll buy another one."

Angus stood up. "Let me talk to her."

Charlotte's face softened. "Oh, Angus, you're my knight in shining armour. Would you?" Then her voice hardened. "Will you tell her to fuck off, and then fuck off some more?"

Angus pushed his glasses up his nose. "I'll find out what she wants, and ask her to remove her car from your property."

Charlotte watched Angus leave the room. She slumped in her chair, then picked up her phone. She had to talk to

Misty; she needed her. It was crisis time. Even though they'd talked about this moment for a long time – a couple of years, in fact – and the importance of her containing her feelings, the moment she'd seen Michelle standing there, everything had come pouring out. She hated herself for it. Why couldn't she control her emotions?

She looked at her phone but waited until Angus came back. Then she paced the room, waiting to hear the front door open. She looked at her watch: it was only a minute since he'd gone out.

She'd managed to avoid meeting Michelle and Idris plenty of times since they'd split up. Their divorce agreement was as amicable as it could be. She'd petitioned for divorce quickly, due to his infidelity, and he'd agreed. The money was split fifty-fifty. They'd both invested the same amount of money when they started the cybersecurity company, and after the set-up period, put an equal amount of hours into it. But it was Charlotte's idea, and she'd pushed the business forward every step of the way. Idris was mouthy and talked the talk, but Charlotte had planned and strategised how to build up the company.

She'd always suspected that Michelle wanted to marry Idris quickly in case he changed his mind. And not just for love either. With the money from the sale of the company, Michelle had not only Charlotte's husband but a cash windfall too. A hundred million each, and Michelle had wanted her share of Idris's half. Charlotte suspected they'd only been friends for so long because Michelle was biding her time to get her claws into Idris – and he'd been stupid enough to oblige.

There was still no sign of Angus, so Charlotte moved into the small living room at the front, stood by the side of the window so as not to be seen, and peeped out. She could see Angus's back. Michelle was standing in front of him, talking, and she kept running her hand through her hair.

Maybe she'd come to apologise.

Maybe Idris had dumped her. For a younger woman, perhaps. She smiled at the thought. Yes, that was probably it. Maybe she should talk to Michelle after all. She'd enjoy hearing how her cheating ex-husband had cheated on Michelle too. She'd have no sympathy for her, and it would be glorious.

Then she heard the front door open and went to the hallway to meet Angus. He looked at her, his expression concerned.

"Has he dumped her? Is she here to apologise?" Charlotte blurted out.

Angus shook his head. "No, but you really need to hear what she has to tell you."

Charlotte sighed. "Et tu, Brute?" she said, quoting the famous line from *Julius Caesar*. Angus had betrayed her too. She felt a rush of pure despair.

He shook his head. "Not at all. It is about Idris, but if you trust me, you need to let her speak to you."

"Of course I trust you." She put her hands on her hips, just as Michelle had done minutes before. "What is it? Has he lost all his money in a dodgy investment?"

"No, it's—"

Charlotte put her hand up. "Don't let her get you to do her dirty work for her. She can tell me herself." She folded her arms.

Angus sighed. "Go into the lounge and I'll bring her in."

Charlotte eyed him. Of course she trusted Angus, but she also knew that Michelle was a devious husband-stealer. Maybe she'd made up some sob story. She took a deep breath and closed her eyes.

7

Angus put his hand on her arm for a moment. "I'll stay with you. You don't have to face her alone." His voice was soft and caring.

Charlotte opened her eyes again, managed a smile, then went into the lounge.

She heard the front door open, then close. Michelle came in, followed by Angus. Charlotte indicated to Angus to sit next to her on the sofa and he moved around Michelle.

"Would you like to take a seat?" he asked Michelle. Charlotte scowled at him, but he didn't react.

Michelle sat down in the chair opposite.

"Whatever you have to say, Michelle, make it quick." Charlotte spoke in a clear, cool tone. She was surprised at her self-control. Her therapist would be proud.

Michelle took a deep breath. "It's Idris. He's been kidnapped."

Chapter Two

"What?" Charlotte let out a small laugh in disbelief.

Michelle stared at her. "I'm serious. He's been kidnapped."

Charlotte narrowed her eyes. "He'll be off with another woman – you do realise that? He used to disappear every so often when I was married to him. He was with his mistress. You."

"He's not with another woman. He's been kidnapped."

"What evidence do you have?"

"The CCTV in the house, and a note they left when they took him. They said if I told the police, they'd kill him." The words gushed out of Michelle.

"Have you told the police?" Angus asked.

"No! That's why I'm here. I don't know what to do."

"So you came here out of desperation." Charlotte folded her arms.

"You're an investigator now, aren't you? Idris said you found a missing boy months ago."

Charlotte and Angus shared a glance. "We did," Angus replied. "What have the kidnappers demanded?"

"The note said one hundred million pounds."

"A hundred million?" Charlotte leaned back on the sofa. "Seriously, who would ask for that amount of money? No one has that in cash, and tracking it would be a piece of cake."

"Well, they did," Michelle snapped back.

Charlotte pondered, then picked up her phone from the coffee table.

"What are you doing?" Michelle demanded, with a frown.

"Phoning the police."

"You can't! They said they'd kill him."

"Exactly," Charlotte replied in a dry tone.

Angus put his hand on Charlotte's arm. "Don't call the police yet. Let's look at the evidence first. But I do think it will be best to call them in the end. If Idris has been taken, he's their leverage. Anyway, all kidnappers threaten to kill their victim if the police are notified. It's a well-known tactic." He turned to Michelle. "Could you let me see the note?"

Michelle picked up her handbag, delved in it, pulled out an A4-sized piece of plain paper and handed it to Angus.

"We have Idris Beavin £100 million or he dies call police he dies", he read aloud, then handed it to Charlotte.

"That's the only message," said Michelle. "They didn't even tell me how to give them the money."

Charlotte tutted. "The lack of proper punctuation is shocking. That suggests someone less than thirty years old. Either English isn't their first language, they're badly educated, or they're trying to look uneducated."

"I thought it was a joke at first," said Michelle. "You know Idris; he's always larking around." She looked at Charlotte. "I phoned his number and it kept going to voice-mail. But last night I phoned again and the kidnapper picked up the phone. It was horrible..." She burst into tears.

Angus took out his notebook and started writing notes, eyeing Michelle every so often to see if her crying had subsided. Charlotte was surprised Michelle was so upset and a wave of guilt went through her. She'd always believed Michelle was simply attracted to Idris's money. She'd learnt afterwards that the affair had started around the time the negotiations to sell their cybersecurity company had begun. They'd told each other everything: they were best friends, after all. Except that Michelle hadn't told her everything. For a year, she'd hidden her affair with Idris.

"He said ... he had Idris," Michelle gasped between sobs, "and I better ... get the money ready ... because time was ... running out. Then the phone went dead."

Charlotte decided this was the most bizarre event that had ever happened to her, and the last thing she'd ever expected.

"I thought it was some troll on the internet trying to be funny. Since he's been on *Vipers' Nest*, loads of crazy people have contacted him. Some of them nice, some not. Idris loves being on that show. He's made for the camera, and helping young entrepreneurs with good ideas has given him a new lease on life."

"Did any of the crazy people stand out?" Angus's pen hovered above the notebook.

Michelle shook her head. "Not really. I was surprised by the amount of vitriol out there. I thought everyone would love him. Especially in Wales, what with him being Welsh, but that couldn't have been further from the truth."

Angus looked up from his notebook. "We'll need to look through all the threats and see if any of them might be the kidnappers."

"Whoa," Charlotte said, looking at Angus. "If he has been kidnapped, we need to let the police know. Even if it's my brother. We are *not* looking for Idris."

Michelle scoffed. "I should have known you'd be like this."

"Like what?"

"Unable to put the past behind you."

"Yeah, well, you stole my husband."

"We loved each other. We still love each other. We couldn't stop our feelings."

"You bitch. Idris and I were married, in case you've forgotten, and you were my best friend!"

"You had no idea what you had." Michelle's chin jutted out.

Charlotte stood up and turned to Angus. "I am not helping her. I don't care what the kidnappers said in their message. I'm calling my brother, Mark. The police can handle this."

Michelle got to her feet and squared up to Charlotte. "You're going to kill him."

Chapter Three

C harlotte laughed, "Don't be ridiculous." She walked to the window and looked out. Her mind was too full of emotion to see anything. "Just go. Pay the ransom and get him back. We'll see how long your relationship lasts when he's penniless. His money was all you were after, wasn't it?"

"God, Charlotte, you're such a stupid bitch. You've been waiting for something like this, haven't you? Some crisis where you can get on your high horse. I knew it was a stupid idea to come here. I should have gone to a proper private investigator."

Charlotte turned round. "Get out."

Angus stood up. "Now come on, both of you. We must put the past *in* the past, for a short time, and find Idris." He turned to Charlotte. "However you feel about him now, you've got to admit that he's in danger. If you can't take this case for Michelle, you should do it for your sons."

The mention of Gethin and Rhys made Charlotte back down. "Do they know?" she asked Michelle, in a softer tone.

"No. They barely talk to me. Gethin can't even be in the same room as me."

Charlotte gave her a smug smile. "What did you expect? You were the reason their mother and father broke up." But the thought of her sons losing their father was the tipping point. She'd known as soon as Michelle told her about the kidnapping that she'd have to help. Most of the arguments running through her head were her fighting her instincts.

Charlotte closed her eyes and took a deep breath, then opened them again. "I will help you find him," she said. "But you'll pay our usual fee, and once he's found, you disappear. I don't want to see you when this is over. I'm starting to move on, and I don't want you ruining that. I'm doing this for my children. Not for you, and not for Idris."

Michelle began to move towards Charlotte, then stopped short. "Thank you."

Angus turned to Michelle. "We need to trace Idris's steps before he was taken. Yesterday and the day before are most important, but tell me anything else that might point to who is behind this."

Michelle nodded.

"And we'll need any laptops, computers or other devices he used. Charlotte will check them."

"I have his iPad and laptop in the car. I'll go and get them."

They watched Michelle leave, then Angus turned to Charlotte. "I think it's better that I take the lead on this. I'll be more objective."

"You always take the lead," Charlotte replied. "You're the one with all the police experience."

"I know, but I want it to be clear from the start because of who we're looking for. And, by the way, you've done the right thing. However badly he treated you, it's the right thing to do. You have to help."

Charlotte gave him a small smile. She knew it, too, but she had already started to feel resentment towards Idris for getting himself in this situation. It had probably happened because he was on TV. Why couldn't he just have gone off to an exotic island and stayed there?

Michelle came back with the devices and handed them to Charlotte. "Do you know any of his passwords?" Charlotte asked her.

Michelle shook her head. "He never told me, and I never asked. I respected his privacy."

"Are you implying that I didn't?" Charlotte opened the laptop.

"No." Michelle sighed. "Is it going to be like this all the time?"

Charlotte met her gaze. "Yep. You broke up my marriage. I may be helping you, but I never promised to be nice."

Michelle huffed, then walked away and sat opposite Angus on the other side of the room. Charlotte felt a wave of self-satisfaction. It was childish, and she knew it, but she was struggling to stop her blood boiling from being in the same room as Michelle.

The last time she'd seen her had been a few weeks after Michelle and Idris had stood in front of her and told her that they were together. That was a horrible memory. They had stood there, arms linked, as Idris said that he didn't love her any more and he was ending their marriage. Michelle was silent, with a smug expression on her face. Charlotte couldn't remember exactly what she'd said – she'd blocked it out – but she remembered the pain of losing her best friend and her husband in the same moment. She closed her eyes and pushed it all away.

She wasn't really listening to the conversation on the opposite side of the room. No doubt Angus was asking Michelle lots of questions about Idris's last movements before he had been taken. At any rate, he was constantly writing in his notepad. Even from across the room she could see his super-neat handwriting, so unlike her own spidery script.

Michelle looked stressed: she was hunched in her seat as she talked, with her hand on her forehead.

She'd have to let Michelle stay in her house, of course. She needed to be around in case the kidnappers contacted her. There were six spare bedrooms, and she'd give Michelle the smallest. The bedrooms were all decorated with exquisite taste, though: far too good for Michelle. Charlotte suddenly wished she had a box room with no window.

Chapter Four

"I need you to go through everything that happened yesterday," Angus said the moment Michelle sat down. "He was taken yesterday morning?"

Michelle nodded.

"I need you to go through everything you remember that morning, right from the moment you woke up."

Michelle sat back in the chair. "I got up at about eight am. Idris was already up: he likes to work out early in our gym. I made us breakfast at about nine am when he'd showered and dressed."

Michelle watched as Angus started writing notes. "Then Idris went to his computer to check his emails and I relaxed in the conservatory, reading. At about ten fifteen, I decided to walk to the local farm shop to get something for lunch later."

"How far is it?"

"Not too far. It takes about twenty minutes, but I like the walk."

"So you were back by...?"

"Ten fifty am: it's on the CCTV. I got back and the

front door was open. That was unusual because Idris is always so careful with security. I looked around the house for him, and that's when I found the ransom note."

Michelle started to cry again. Angus looked around, saw a box of tissues on the table near Charlotte and retrieved it.

Michelle took one. "Thank you."

"Just continue when you are ready." Angus stopped writing. From his time in the police, he'd interviewed hundreds of people and knew when to pause to give them a moment.

Michelle nodded and dabbed her eyes with the tissue. "I phoned him, but it went to voicemail. Then I used that app on my phone. You know, the one you can use to track someone's location."

Angus glanced at Charlotte, but she didn't flinch or show any sign of having heard. He was sure that she was still tracking *his* phone with a similar app. "And what did it say?"

"The app just said it couldn't find his location."

"They must have switched his phone off the moment they took him." Angus made a note to check with Charlotte whether there was any other reason why Idris's phone might have no location. "Had he received any threats recently?"

Michelle shot him a scornful look. "Bloody hell, yeah. He's got tons of fans now that he's on *Vipers' Nest*, but he's had some right nasty people contacting him too. They say things like he's a disgrace to Wales or he should only be investing in Welsh entrepreneurs – that type of thing. They're mainly anonymous, with anime avatars. He joined TikTok recently – all the kids are using that – and he loved coming up with little skits to post on there. I was in some of them."

Charlotte looked up, incredulous. "TikTok? For goodness' sake."

"It's fun, and we get lots of likes. Idris played a prank on me last week and uploaded it. It went viral, with two hundred thousand likes."

Charlotte shook her head. "Well, if you want to let him humiliate you in front of the world, that's your prerogative. For your information, he has a track record of humiliating his wives."

There was a long silence until Angus cleared his throat. "Did anyone stand out? Were there any threats to kidnap him? Any death threats, even?"

"No. Lots of people pitching ideas to him, and lots of begging letters. God, it was endless."

"Good luck to them," Charlotte said coolly. "He wouldn't have a clue about what works – or doesn't."

Michelle stared at her. She didn't say anything, though, and Charlotte took that as an acknowledgement that she was right.

Angus thought for a moment. "When you got home, was there any sign of a disturbance either in the house or outside?"

"Just that the front door was open, and the note."

"You realised straight away that something was wrong?"

"Yeah. That's when I checked the CCTV cameras and saw he'd been taken."

"Have you got the CCTV recording?" Angus asked.

"Yes, I downloaded it onto a flash drive. I knew you'd need to see it."

She delved into her handbag and took out her keys. On the chain was the drive. She handed it to Angus, and he took it to Charlotte.

Charlotte left the room to retrieve her laptop, and on

her return plugged in the drive. After a few clicks of her mouse, the recording began. The camera was pointing from what Charlotte presumed was a special hole in the front door, and showed the driveway and the space just in front of the door.

Charlotte glanced at Michelle. "This is your house in Hertfordshire?"

"Yes, we moved there a year ago." Charlotte had heard about the house from Rhys, her youngest son: it was a small mansion in West Hertfordshire.

The video showed a black transit-style van pulling up outside. A man wearing black jeans, a black T-shirt and a balaclava got out of the driver's side and rang the doorbell. He looked average height, and probably less than forty. When the door opened, he pointed a handgun at Idris and motioned at him with the gun to move. A few moments later, Idris came into view, his hands up as he was led to the van. The man pushed Idris against the side of the van, put handcuffs on him, then shoved him into the back and slammed the door. He walked through the front door, stopped in the hall and looked around, then went off screen. About a minute later, he walked out carrying Idris's phone, leaving the front door open, got into the van and drove off.

"Is there no sound?" Charlotte asked.

"No. Idris didn't want it; he just wanted the video."

They watched it again, but this time Charlotte paused the video to get the van's registration number, make and model.

"It's bound to be a fake, but we need to eliminate it from the investigation." Angus wrote the registration down, then searched for it using his phone.

Charlotte looked at him, impressed. "You know, it's

great to see you using technology more and more in your everyday life."

Angus raised an eyebrow at her, then checked his phone. "According to the DVLA website, that's a red Vauxhall Astra. They probably stole the plates and put them on, or used illicit means to get them printed."

"We could find where the car is registered. That might be a clue?"

Angus nodded. "It's worth looking at. It's probably a random choice, or a case of what was available, but you never know."

"I'll see what I can find as soon as I've looked at his laptop and iPad."

"I'll get my police contact to find the address. That way you'll have more time to go through Idris's accounts."

Charlotte smiled. "So you still have lots of ex-colleagues who owe you favours?"

"You have no idea."

Charlotte stretched her arms above her head. "By the way, I've got into his laptop."

"Already?" Michelle asked.

"Yep, I'm really good. Cracked his password in thirteen seconds. It's 'cyfrinair': 'password' in Welsh. Absolutely reckless to pick something so obvious. It's almost as if he knows nothing about cybersecurity." She glanced at Angus, and the corner of his mouth turned up a little.

"I've got into his tablet too," Charlotte added. "I tried his year of birth, which let me in straight away. He wasn't even trying to keep it secure. I'll go through his emails now..." She gave Angus a pointed look.

Angus took the hint to leave her alone and returned to the sofa and Michelle.

Charlotte opened Idris's emails and began to look

through them. It felt weird. She'd never read his emails when they were married; they'd always respected each other's privacy. Maybe she should have read them, and then she'd have found out earlier about his affair with Michelle.

When they'd sold their company, they'd both had to sign an agreement that they wouldn't work in cybersecurity for five years, or start a new company in that field. At the time, it had been an easy decision for them both because they'd planned to see the world together. They could see all the countries they'd talked about visiting when they were students and could barely afford the bus fare to the campus. They'd lain awake at night talking about America, Asia, Canada, India…

Charlotte pushed the thought aside. She had to get over her feelings and crack on with the job at hand. Instead of reminiscing, she could think about how smug she'd be when she found him. She imagined the look on his face as the realisation dawned that he owed her big time. That pushed her motivation levels sky-high, and she focused on her screen, determined to find a clue.

Chapter Five

Angus looked at his notes. The hours before Idris's disappearance were starting to become clear. Kidnappings were usually well organised, but they weren't always undertaken solely for money. During his time in the police, Angus had dealt with a gang member who'd been kidnapped by a rival gang. Unfortunately for the victim, they'd come across his decaying body weeks after he'd been reported missing.

He looked at Michelle. "Could Idris have been kidnapped to force you or him to do something?"

"What do you mean?"

"Was there something that Idris had been refusing to do?"

Michelle shook her head. "Not that I can think of. I'm sure it's just for the money."

Angus's phone rang and he glanced at the display. He was half-expecting it to be Charlotte, phoning from across the room, but his eyebrows shot up at the caller's name: Duncan, his big brother, whom he hadn't spoken to in ages.

Their last contact had been at Christmas, when they'd

all gathered in their parents' house in Stirling. They weren't particularly close now that they were older, since Duncan had moved back to Scotland as soon as he was old enough, decades ago. He was in his mid-fifties, only two years older than Angus, and lived in one of the nicer parts of Edinburgh. It was unlike Duncan to call, so that meant he needed to answer it.

"Sorry, I need to get this." Angus stood up and walked into the hallway. "Duncan, how are you? It's nice to hear from you."

The voice at the end of the line sounded crisp and clear as though Duncan were in the next room. "Hello, little brother. I'm good, thanks. How are things in sunny Devon?"

"Not very sunny at the moment, but I'm sure it's warmer than where you are." Angus suppressed a shiver. Whenever he visited Scotland, the temperature difference was profound. Being three hundred miles north of Devon produced a stark contrast in the weather. It was one of the reasons why he loved Devon so much.

There was a brief pause before Duncan spoke again. "Look, I need a favour."

"Sure. Is it Mum and Dad?"

"No, no, nothing like that. It's Euan."

Euan was Duncan's son and Angus's nephew. Angus thought for a moment: he must be nearly seventeen. "Sure, what is it?"

"Well, you see, he's failed all his higher exams. That's because he's starting to get a bit out of hand. Mixing with the wrong crowd, if you understand what I mean."

"How can I help?" Angus asked. He wasn't sure what he could do, especially as he wasn't in the police any more and so far away. Give him a talking-to over the phone, maybe.

"Would you have him stay for a wee while? A month or so would do it. I need to get him away from these bad influences so he doesn't get into trouble."

Angus let out a breath: he hadn't expected that. "Yeah, sure, I guess. When were you thinking of?"

"I'm about fifteen minutes away from your house. We're parked at the M5 services just outside Exeter."

Angus's emotions swung from being glad to see Duncan and worry that he had come all that way without checking if it was okay for him to stay.

"Okay..." Angus rubbed his forehead, thinking. "I'm out at the moment, but I can come back. It will take me about twenty minutes. I'm in Topsham."

He ended the call and went back into the room. "Sorry, but I've got to go home for a short time. Family emergency."

Charlotte looked up. "Anything I can help with?"

"Not at the moment, but I may take you up on that. My nephew is coming to stay for a few weeks. I might have to bring him with me." He turned to Michelle. "I'll be back as soon as I can. In the meantime, if the kidnappers contact you, call me straight away." He picked up his notebook. "Try not to kill each other while I'm gone."

When Angus arrived at his suburban semi-detached home, in a leafy part of Exeter, he looked around the living room. The house was clean, and he could put Euan in one of the two spare bedrooms. There wasn't much food in, but he could order takeaway tonight and get supplies tomorrow.

The doorbell rang, interrupting his thoughts. Angus took a deep breath and went to the door. He was always pleased to see his brother and couldn't suppress a smile when he opened the door.

Duncan was standing there alone. "I know it was presumptuous, but I knew you'd not say no."

Angus stepped outside and the two men hugged briefly. "It's good to see you." Angus took a step back and looked at Duncan. He clearly wasn't sleeping well: there were dark patches under his eyes. And judging by the length of his stubble, he hadn't shaved for a while.

Angus looked at the car parked outside his house. Euan was in the passenger seat, his face like a recently slapped backside. "Is he coming in?"

Duncan glanced over. "He says not, but he's not coming back home either."

"You go in; I'll see if I can get him out of the car."

Duncan nodded and retreated inside the house.

Angus opened the driver's door and got into the car. Euan kept looking forward, saying nothing. He'd grown since the last time Angus had seen him: he was adult-size now. His hair was carefully styled into a trendy side brushup. His cheeks were spattered with teenage acne and he was dressed in a navy-blue hoody and jeans.

"My favourite nephew! How are you, Euan? It's good to see you."

Euan glanced briefly at Angus. "I'm your only nephew."

"Still my favourite, though." No response. "So, are you going to come in? It's been a long trip for you."

"No."

Angus sighed. "Look, whatever's happened, you should come in and at least get something to eat and drink. Your dad wants you to stay here with me for a while. Is that so bad?"

Euan shrugged. "I'm not hungry. We've just been to the services."

Angus paused for a moment. "Well, you can't stay in here. How long did it take you to drive down?"

Euan shrugged.

"Last time I drove back, it took me eleven hours with a couple of stops. You must be fed up with the inside of the car."

Euan gave him a sideways glance.

Angus ran his hand over his face. "Look, I know your dad can be an annoying bastard at times. I should know: he was the bane of my life for years. But his heart's in the right place. Come on in. Once he's gone, we can compare notes."

Euan looked at him, and cracked a small smile.

Chapter Six

Charlotte was determined not to tell her sons about the kidnapping. Not yet, anyway. She didn't want to worry them this early on, not while they were busy studying. She hadn't found anything of interest in Idris's emails. There was a plethora of marketing emails from companies and not much else.

In fact, there were hardly any emails at all. Somehow he'd managed to escape getting piles of spam. Even his deleted emails were sparse. She wondered if he had a different email address. This was the same one he'd had when they were married: iddy@gmail.com. Iddy was what his mother always called him.

She spent a few minutes checking his browser history to see if there was a web-based email, but there was no sign of another email anywhere.

Having dismissed the emails, Charlotte examined Idris's social media accounts. First, she logged into his Facebook profile. He hadn't posted for over six months, and before that it was just boasting about being on TV. There were a few direct messages – some names she recognised, some she didn't – all congratulating him on his performance on *Vipers' Nest*.

Next was Instagram. Charlotte shook her head when she saw that he'd been verified with a blue tick. "I bet you loved that," she found herself saying out loud.

He posted more on there, usually once or twice a week. There were a number of photos of him backstage on *Vipers' Nest*. One showed the main entrance to the studios and was labelled "The Newest Viper Returns". Another showed his dressing-room door, with a printed sign on it that read "Viper: Idris". Just visible in the bottom-right corner was his hand, signalling a thumbs-up.

Charlotte let out a sigh. Just like him. Idris had always been a blagger, wanting people to envy him. He'd always wanted the biggest house and the best car, even if it meant endless loans and mortgages. They'd moved house four times in the eighteen years they'd been married, each time because Idris had wanted a bigger, better house. There had been a larger mortgage every time, too, and despite Idris always telling Charlotte not to worry about money, she had constantly fretted that they wouldn't have enough each month. Somehow they always scraped it together, but she'd had to be thrifty. They hadn't spent much on anything except their mortgage or car loan and the kids. Idris had always wanted to go on exotic holidays, too, but they'd never been able to afford anything other than a fortnight in the Canary Islands.

Charlotte continued scrolling through Idris's Instagram feed. There was a photo of Idris behind a studio camera, pointing it at one of the other Vipers, Stuart Fielder, who'd been in the show since the start, standing in a stupid pose: one arm in the air and his hips to the side.

She pushed aside her dismay at such a stupid photo,

and loaded a web-scraping program that would go through each photo and download the comments. Then she could see if any were threatening, or came from persistent posters.

It took a few minutes, but there were plenty of candidates. Lots of comments of adulation, lots from Welsh people, grateful, as one stated, "that he was smashing the stereotypes of Welshmen", whatever that meant. There were a few flirty comments from women, but the direct messages yielded the most potential candidates.

Some were just simple messages from members of the public: "Love ya", "Nice to see a Welshman on the TV", "You're a breath of fresh air".

Others were more persistent. One man messaged him while watching each episode, commenting on what Idris had said. Idris never answered, but he'd read the messages. Nothing indicated that this man would up his game and kidnap Idris, though.

Finally, there was TikTok. He'd posted some promotional videos for products he'd decided to invest in, such as a craft-beer company with a myriad of low or non-alcoholic options. That didn't surprise her. Idris's father had been a drinker back in the day, and Idris had told her about lost days out and money worries when he was a child.

Then there was the prank video Michelle had mentioned. It showed him presenting Michelle with a jewellery box, and her smiling and accepting it. When she opened it, out jumped a fake spider. She screamed, he laughed, then they both almost fell over laughing.

There was only one more thing to do: look at the people Idris had blocked on his social media.

On Facebook, Charlotte was surprised to see that one of the first people in the list was her. "Stupid bastard," she said flatly. It hadn't even crossed her mind that he'd block her on Facebook. She hardly used it anyway.

Michelle looked up.

"He's blocked me on Facebook," said Charlotte.

Michelle shrugged. "He just wanted to move on, you know?"

Charlotte straightened up. "Well, if he wants to move on from me, I can stop right now." She moved her chair away from the computer.

Michelle grimaced. "Not like that. You know what I mean."

Charlotte went back to work. She couldn't stop herself from glancing at Michelle every now and again, though. Michelle had stolen her husband and had an affair with him for over a year before they admitted to it. It was no wonder she'd been such a mess. She'd been inconsolable for months. Fiona, her sister-in-law, and Helena her housekeeper and friend had been her rocks during that dark time.

When Charlotte had found out about Michelle and Idris's affair, she'd been clueless, but in hindsight, she should have seen what was going on. Idris was spending more time at home, especially when Michelle was there. Michelle would say she had to go, and shortly afterwards Idris would leave, saying he'd been asked out for the night by a friend. How had she not seen it?

Idris had blocked plenty of fans on every social media platform. Most were on Twitter, but that wasn't surprising, as it was where he'd received most abuse. People on there seemed to think they could say things they'd never say to someone in real life.

It took Charlotte a while, but she identified a few accounts which had messaged him repeatedly. They got quite nasty at times, and started new accounts as soon as

Idris blocked them. The avatar and name was different, but the IP address was the same. Yet nothing indicated they would take things further.

Charlotte considered posting something from Idris's Twitter account. She could post something that would make him look really stupid. Maybe that Charlotte had thought up the business idea, or that he had had an affair behind his then-wife's back. She forced the thought from her mind. That would be childish, however tempting it was.

An hour later, she had two people, both from Twitter, who were prime candidates. Neither had used their real names in their profiles, but it had been easy enough to work out their identities from their other social media accounts, which had the same or similar names.

She got out her conspiracy board and started to pin things to it. First a picture of Idris, with the word "Kidnapped" underneath, then the two social media suspects.

It wasn't much to go on, and she hoped Angus would have some ideas of what to look into next. She wondered how his brother and nephew were, and whether their arrival would have much impact on the investigation.

Angus pushed a cup of tea across the kitchen bench to his brother. Duncan was sitting in the chair normally occupied by Charlotte. He looked tired and stressed, and his hair was greyer than the last time they'd seen each other.

Duncan took a sip and rubbed his eyes. "That's just what I needed. Thanks."

"You must have driven all night."

"We did. I had to get him away."

"What happened?"

"He's been getting in with the wrong crowd."

"That's normal at his age. What is it? Drugs? Alcohol?"

Duncan put the cup down carefully. "No – nothing more than a bottle of Buckfast wine now and again. He's started hanging out with the local graffiti artists, except it's not really art, it's tagging. He was caught by the police last week and they gave him a warning, but he's been out doing it again. He's got an Instagram account where he posts photos of it."

"I don't like graffiti, but it's not that bad, is it? Does he want to be an artist?"

"I don't think so: he's not even taking it at school. Dropped it as soon as he could. He's always shown more interest in computers."

That wasn't as bad as Angus had feared. "Are they up to anything else?"

"Not as far as I know. I should be thankful, I suppose. But they've been egging each other on to tag more and more prominent places around Edinburgh. They were building up to tagging the Scottish Parliament."

Angus nearly spat out his tea and just suppressed a laugh. "They do realise it has armed police and facial-recognition CCTV?"

"Yeah, that was the challenge. I've taken his phone off him so he can detox."

"Good idea."

"Bit different from what we got up to, though." Duncan's eyes brightened and a smile spread over his face.

"What, drinking a few cans and hanging out in Belmont Park?"

"Those were the days."

"Every time I go past Belmont, I think about you and Naomi Jones snogging behind the Scout hut," Angus reminisced.

Duncan laughed. "That didn't last long."

"She came to her senses." Angus grinned.

Duncan took another sip of tea. "I appreciate you taking him in. He'll be back at school for retakes in a few weeks, and hopefully the ones he's been hanging out with will have gone."

"I'll look after him, never fear." Angus looked at his watch. "Look, I can't hang around. As much as I'd like to catch up, I have something big going on at work. Why don't you get some kip and I'll see you later. Stay the night, at least."

"I don't want to cause extra hassle."

"It's not hassle, but I need to get back to work. It's time-sensitive. I can't talk about it, I'm afraid."

"Sounds intriguing. Will Euan be in the way?"

Angus wanted to say yes, but he also wanted to help his brother and nephew. "Not at all. He can help with the case if he wants something to occupy his time." He wasn't sure how, but Charlotte would come up with something.

As though he'd known they were talking about him, Euan emerged at the kitchen door with a long face.

Angus had been leaning against the kitchen worktop and he pushed himself upright. "I know you said you'd been to the services, Euan, but how about something now? I've got some really nice triple-chocolate biscuits..."

Euan shrugged. It wasn't a no, so Angus opened the cupboard, took out the packet and handed it to him.

"I'll have one too." Duncan reached for the packet, opened it and bit into one. "Mmm, that is really nice."

Euan brightened after he'd eaten four biscuits and went off to watch TV. Angus looked at his watch. "Are you okay for now, Duncan?"

Duncan stretched his arms above his head and yawned.

"Yeah, yeah, you go. I'll go lie down for a wee while and see you later. If I'm up to it, I'll get Euan out and show him some of the places we used to hang around."

"If I wasn't dealing with something urgent, I'd come with you."

Chapter Seven

A ngus returned to Charlotte's house. Michelle and Charlotte were in her living room. Charlotte had put Idris's iPad and laptop on the far table, and next to it her conspiracy board, with a photo of him in the middle.

She pointed to the board. "I have two possible suspects in social media. They looked crazy enough to take things further." She pointed to a printout of a question mark. "MadMax567 is Simon Smith, in his thirties, from Cardiff. From his social media posts, he's an opinionated trouble-maker who goes out of his way to be nasty to people on Twitter. Most of his followers are similar. However, this sort of trolling behaviour on Twitter isn't unusual."

Charlotte pointed to the other profile. "TriggerTrou-bleLOL is another male who likes to send spiteful messages to celebrities on the internet. His real name is Nigel Smith. He lives in Norwich and he's a flat-earther, climate-change denier, etcetera. He's got his own YouTube channel. To be honest, he looks too interested in other things to bother with Idris."

"Why is he on the board, then?" asked Angus.

"Because he's threatened Idris multiple times. For example..." She picked up a piece of paper. "I would love to smash your stupid Welsh face in, you f**ing leek muncher." She tilted her head and blinked. "Admittedly, he's not the only one who'd like to do that to him."

Angus took a deep breath. "Okay, one in Norwich, one in Cardiff. Which do we go for first?"

Michelle cleared her throat. "I'm no geography expert, but won't it take hours and hours to get to Norwich?"

"At least five to six hours, if there are no hold-ups," said Angus. "Cardiff will take a few hours. There are always terrible tailbacks north of Bristol, at Cribbs Causeway shopping centre. It's a nightmare."

Charlotte raised an eyebrow. "You shop at Cribbs Causeway a lot, then?"

Angus pushed his glasses up. "I have been known to, yes. It's a nice change from Exeter. The selection of menswear shops is more extensive." He pulled at his tie. "We haven't got time to go to Cardiff, and we can't possibly visit Norwich on a hunch."

Charlotte pondered. "What if we could get to Cardiff and Norwich quickly?"

"Like how? Helicopter?" Angus laughed, then his eyes widened. "You've got a helicopter?"

"No, but I know someone who has. You can hire them."

"Won't that cost a lot of money?" Angus asked.

Charlotte looked at Michelle. "It would go on the bill. Expenses."

Michelle shrugged. "I just want Idris back. If that means hiring a helicopter, I'll pay."

Angus folded his arms. "I think it's better if we send Grigore. He can check them both out and report back.

Despite being on the board, they're a long shot, and it's mainly for elimination purposes." It was more an instruction than an opinion.

"All right. We can brief Grigore, and I'll make sure he has a car waiting at the helipads." She picked up her phone, scrolled through the contacts and clicked the screen. "Hello, my love, it's Charlotte. How are you? Yes, very well, thank you. You're such a sweetie to ask. Look, I need your help. That favour you owe me: I'm calling it in. I need your chopper. Are you free today?"

It turned out that the helicopter owner was free. After a few minutes of Charlotte explaining what they'd planned, she hung up and went to find Grigore, who nodded as they described what he needed to do. When Grigore had left, they returned to the conspiracy board.

"When did the kidnappers say they'd contact you again?" Charlotte asked Michelle.

"They didn't. It could be any time." Michelle looked at her mobile phone, lying on the sofa, which showed no messages. "I've been checking every minute. It's got a signal, but there's been nothing." She frowned. "If Idris even had a hundred million pounds in cash, wouldn't it be difficult to carry? I mean, even in fifty-pound notes..."

"They won't want cash, they'll want cryptocurrency," said Charlotte. "I'm sure of it."

"Really?" Michelle asked.

"Absolutely. How else will they keep under the radar? Cash is so last century."

"Stupid bastards. I can't believe someone would do this. They're just jealous of his money." Michelle started to sob again, and Angus noticed a flash of empathy in Charlotte's face. No doubt she was trying to reconcile not consoling Michelle with the fact that she'd stolen her husband.

Michelle's sobbing was interrupted by her phone ringing. They all looked at each other, then Michelle looked at the screen. "It's a blocked number. It must be the kidnappers."

Angus nodded to her to answer. She picked up the phone with a trembling hand and put it on speakerphone.

After a moment of silence, a deep male voice with a London accent spoke. "If you want to see him again, purchase an NFT. I'll text you the link. Ten million to start, just to make sure you're playing ball. I'll tell you where to send it in six hours." The call ended.

"Wait, what?" Michelle looked completely blank. "NFT? What was he talking about? What's an NFT?"

Charlotte rolled her eyes. "Hasn't Idris taught you anything? NFT: Non-Fungible Token. It's similar to cryptocurrency, but you buy a digital object instead of a physical one. People are selling all sorts of crazy things. Electronic drawings – most of which look as if a five-year-old did them, digital first editions of books, and some football clubs are selling unique digital assets."

"Why would they want me to buy a digital asset?"

"Because they're often used to launder money. Put a blank painting on sale for millions. Someone buys it and everyone thinks they're stupid, but it's just a way of legitimising money from things like drugs and prostitution."

"They want to get the money via crypto, just like you said," Angus stated.

"Yep. I love being right."

Michelle put a palm to her forehead. "But I haven't got access to ten million pounds. I've only got a few hundred thousand in my account. Charlotte, you'll have to pay."

Charlotte's mouth fell open. "Me? I haven't got quick access to that type of money either. Besides, you should never pay ransoms. And as I said earlier, I can't see why they would kill their only leverage. They must be up to something."

Angus studied the conspiracy board. "I agree with Charlotte: there's no way they'll kill him. Not until they have the money, that is. We need to tell the police."

Michelle shook her head. "We've been over this. We can't tell them – we just can't! I don't know what I'd do without him."

Charlotte joined Angus. "Was there anyone at *Vipers' Nest* who might have done this?"

Michelle frowned. "I don't think so."

"Did he get on with everyone?"

"Yeah. I mean, it was always going to be a battle of egos with all those multimillionaires in one room. The bragging was unbelievable at times. Idris felt he needed to prove himself to them. He suffered from imposter syndrome, I'm sure. He never admitted it, but I could tell."

"I can imagine it was a nightmare," said Angus. He took a piece of A4 paper and a black marker pen and made a list of the other Vipers, which he stuck on the board.

Charlotte stared at him. "How do you know the names of all the Vipers?"

Angus shrugged. "I usually stream the show on the computer a few nights after it's broadcast."

Charlotte stood there, mouth open, unable to pull together her thoughts. Eventually, she spoke. "Have you always watched it, or did you start watching because my ex-husband is in it?"

Angus put his hands in his pockets. "I started watching because of Idris. I thought I'd give it a try, and discovered I liked it."

Charlotte grabbed the side of the chair and sat down.

"Well, that is a surprise. You've been watching it all this time and you never mentioned it." There was a sort of anguish in her voice.

"He probably didn't say anything because he realised you'd get arsey with him, like you are now," Michelle commented.

Charlotte glared at her. "I'm not getting arsey, I just had no idea."

"I'm allowed to watch what I like, you know." Angus gave Charlotte a *you know I'm right* type of look. "I'd never watched it before, but I like it. It's a good programme and the stakes are high for everyone." He turned to Michelle. "Were there any Vipers Idris didn't get on with?"

"He said he liked them all. Magnus Armstrong was a bit aloof at the start and not very welcoming. At first, Sally Hicks didn't talk to him much and was pretty rude, but after a few days, she got quite pally with him. He had a lark about with Stuart. He got on best with Greg Bowman, but over the last couple of weeks, they'd fallen out, and things had been tense during filming."

"Do you know why that was?" Angus asked.

"Yeah." She glanced at Charlotte. "Idris advised him about cryptocurrency investment and it went wrong. He lost some money. I'm not sure how much, but at least a million."

"I don't like the sound of that." Angus shook his head. "It's not ten million, though. From what I've read, Greg Bowman is worth at least a hundred and fifty million pounds – and that's a conservative estimate. He could be spiteful, though. Men like him don't get so successful without being cut-throat, so we can't rule him out. Put him on the board." Charlotte wrote his name on a piece of paper and pinned it to the conspiracy board. "Were there any messages between them?"

Michelle shrugged. "I don't think so; they used to actually phone and speak to each other. Idris still prefers to talk rather than use instant messages."

Charlotte nodded. "Yeah, he always hated texting."

Angus turned to Michelle. "We need to speak to Greg. Do you have his number?"

She shook her head.

Charlotte walked over to Idris's laptop. "I'll check this: his contacts should be on there."

A few minutes later, Charlotte handed a piece of paper to Angus, with Greg's number on it. He shook his head. "He'll be more receptive if you call."

Charlotte's eyes narrowed. "Why?"

Angus tried not to smile. "He has a reputation as a ladies' man."

Charlotte sighed. "I suppose you know that from watching *Vipers' Nest*?" She dialled the number and put it on speakerphone.

After three rings, Greg picked up. "Who is this?" he demanded.

Charlotte put on her most feminine-sounding voice. "Hello, Mr Bowman. My name is Charlotte Lockwood and I'm here with Idris Beavin's wife. She's wondering if you've seen him recently?"

"What? Who?"

"Idris's wife, Michelle. She's here with me."

Michelle bent towards the phone. "Er, hello, this is Michelle. You haven't seen Idris, have you?"

"Idris? No, love, all I've seen is turtles and flamingos. I'm on Necker Island with my mate Rick at the moment. Been here a few weeks, actually. The wildlife is *amazing*."

"He's not with you, then?"

"Fat chance I'd spend any more time with that tosser than I have to. No offence." He laughed. "I'm sure he'll turn up. And when you do see him, tell him he owes me a few hundred grand."

The call ended and they sat silent for a moment.

"Even if he's abroad, that doesn't mean it's not him," said Angus. "He wouldn't do something like this himself: he'd get someone to do his dirty work for him." He sighed. "We need to check he really is abroad, but for now we have to take his word for it."

"I'll check his social media for evidence." Charlotte walked over to her laptop and started typing.

They were interrupted by the sound of the front door opening, then closing.

Helena, Charlotte's friend and housekeeper, appeared in the doorway. Helena was a little older than Charlotte and was from Romania. She wore a pale-blue sleeveless sports top and skinny jeans. Her long brown hair was tied in a ponytail. "Hello, Charlotte, how are—" She saw Michelle and her eyes widened in horror. "Vat *she* do here?"

"Idris has been kidnapped," Charlotte explained. "Michelle is here because she's asked me and Angus to find him."

"Kidnap?" Helena made a sort of scoffing sound. "Really?" She looked at Angus for confirmation.

He nodded. "Apparently so."

She narrowed her eyes and stared at Michelle. "I hope zey kill him."

Michelle gasped.

"He bastard, and you bitch. She has cheek to come here. I no cook for her!" She stabbed her index finger at Michelle.

"It's all right, you don't have to," Charlotte soothed.

Helena shook her head at Charlotte. "You lost your mind."

"Yes, I think I probably have."

Charlotte gave Angus a *help me* look and he stood up. "I'll tell you all about it," he said, leading Helena into the kitchen.

"I can't eat, anyway. Not while he's missing," Michelle said, once they were out of the room.

Charlotte sighed. At one time, before they split up, she'd have been the same.

They heard the distant noise of Helena taking out pots and crockery, then a crash as a pot fell on the floor and Helena swearing in Romanian.

A few minutes later, Angus returned. "Any sign of the NFT?"

Michelle checked her phone. "No. And like I said earlier, I can't buy an NFT for ten million pounds. I don't have access to that sort of money."

"I don't either: at least, not quickly," said Charlotte. "And honestly, even if I did, I don't think it's the right thing to do. Mark told me once that the very worst thing you can do is pay a ransom."

Angus nodded in agreement.

Charlotte continued with her point. "It's the same online with all those ransomware viruses. If everyone stopped paying, hackers would stop using them."

"This isn't the same. Viruses don't threaten to kill someone!" Michelle looked daggers at her.

Charlotte turned to Angus. "I really hope we find Idris quickly. I'm not sure how long I can put up with her."

"You're so rude," Michelle complained.

Charlotte turned back to Michelle. "I'd rather be rude than a husband stealer."

Angus moved between them. "Can you at least be civil while I'm gone home to check on Euan and Duncan?"

Charlotte and Michelle looked at each other. After a moment, they both nodded.

Half an hour after Angus left, Charlotte's phone rang.

"Hello Grigore, how is it going?" The background noise meant he was near the helicopter.

"First I call on Simon Smith in Cardiff. He mature student at university."

"What's he studying?"

"Gender studies." Grigore snorted.

"Good grief."

"He waste of time. He live in bedsit with six others. He passed out on bed from night before. Others say he take drugs, partying all time. He no kidnapper. Next, I call on Nigel in Norwich. He work in dodgy wineshop, and he no kidnapper either. He live with mother and father still. He nobody, he does nothing. Don't zink he could do anything without his mother help."

"Why are all these internet trolls like that?" It was a rhetorical question. Charlotte had been a big fan of the internet since the moment she'd discovered it at university. But the downside was that it allowed the dregs of humanity to have a mouthpiece.

"Are you coming back now?"

"Yez. I love fly."

"Would you like lessons?"

"Yez." He laughed.

Charlotte couldn't help smiling. "Find somewhere that does them and I'll sort it."

"You best boss, Charlotte."

"Flattery will get you everywhere."

"Sorry kidnapper no zem."

"Back to the drawing board..."

"He still kidnapped?"

"Yep, and nothing from the kidnappers either."

"If you need me to go in helicopter again, I ready."

"Thank you so much for doing this, Grigore. You're an absolute star."

Charlotte ended the call. It was disappointing neither of the men were behind the kidnap. It had been a long shot, and she thought through the different posts and direct messages on Idris's social media. Had she made a mistake and missed someone? She decided to go through it all one last time, just to make sure and to keep her mind off having Michelle in the house.

Chapter Eight

When Angus got home he found Duncan asleep on the sofa and Euan watching TV. The sound of Angus coming in woke Duncan, and it took him a moment to remember where he was.

Angus flopped down on the settee next to him. "Get up to anything exciting while I was away?"

"Dad fell asleep," Euan said, folding his arms.

Duncan rubbed his eyes. "Sorry, it was the long drive. It's been a while since I've driven that far."

"It's a long way," said Angus, "especially without stopping."

Euan picked up the remote control and flicked through the channels. "Boring too."

"I'll order a takeaway for dinner," said Angus, ignoring Euan's remark. "I'm used to cooking just for myself, so I've not got much in. Pizza okay?"

"Fine by me." Duncan smiled. "They have pizza delivery in Devon, then?"

"Only since you left."

In the kitchen, Duncan sat on the breakfast barstool while Angus ordered pizza on his phone.

"You're getting very technical." Duncan waved a hand at the phone. "You used to hate technology."

"I still do, but it has its uses." Angus put the phone down. "It'll be about half an hour. You going to head back tomorrow morning?"

"Yeah. I'll leave after rush hour, so I should be home by the evening. I'm sorry to dump him on you like this, but he's always looked up to you. I'm hoping your good influence will rub off on him."

Angus grinned. "Such flattery, big brother. Were things that desperate? Maybe he just needs a change of scene."

"Maybe. Anyway, I've taken his phone off him till he comes back home. It wasn't easy. He wasn't willing to give it up, so I took it when he was asleep."

"Harsh."

"Had to be done. So if he needs to talk to me, it'll have to be via the landline or your phone."

"Got it."

Forty-five minutes later, they were all sitting around the dining-room table. Angus offered Euan another piece of pizza. Like a typical teenage boy, he'd eaten loads, and he'd got more talkative the more he consumed.

Duncan rubbed his stomach. "You can't beat pizza."

The doorbell rang. "Are you expecting someone?" Duncan asked.

"No, but I think I know who it is." Angus wondered if Charlotte had brought Michelle with her.

When he opened the door, there she was. He should have been annoyed, but as soon as he saw the smile on her face, all thoughts of that dissipated. He glanced behind her: there was no sign of Michelle.

Charlotte stepped into the house before he had asked her in. "I've come to update you about Grigore." She headed for the dining room before he had a chance to stop her.

Angus followed her. "Hello, I'm Charlotte," she said, offering her hand to Duncan.

Duncan had been pouring himself another glass of wine. He stood up to shake Charlotte's hand, looking rather surprised at the attractive blonde in front of him.

"And you must be Euan. Hello."

Euan nodded, his eyes wide.

Charlotte looked at the cluster of pizza boxes in front of her. "Oooh, pizza, yummy." She looked at Angus.

"Would you like some?"

"Definitely." She smiled. "Life's too short to refuse pizza."

Duncan gave Angus a questioning look.

"Charlotte works with me," Angus explained. "Come into the kitchen, Charlotte, and you can update me there."

Charlotte reluctantly followed him into the kitchen, holding her piece of pizza. Angus went to a cupboard and pulled out a plate, handing it to her. "Before you start," he said, "is it wise to leave Helena and Michelle alone together?"

"Oh dear, I didn't think of that. I'd better make this quick... Anyway, Grigore phoned." She told him all about the two men he'd looked into. "I know it was a long shot. I guess I should have known they'd just be nobodies who enjoy sending abusive messages on the internet."

"That's why I stay away from social media as much as possible."

"I hardly post on Facebook any more," Charlotte said, a touch defensively. "I pop on Instagram now and again to see what my sons are up to, but nothing else really. What should we do next?"

Angus leant against the kitchen counter. "Have the kidnappers contacted Michelle again?"

"Not yet. Don't you think that's suspicious?"

Angus frowned. "In what way?"

"Wouldn't they want the money A-S-A-P? Why wait?"

"Until we know who they are, we can only speculate. We need to tell the police."

Charlotte pondered his statement for a moment. "I agree. When I get home I'll talk to Michelle, but she'll still want to delay."

"Do what you can."

There was a long pause. "So, how are things with your brother and nephew?"

"Fine."

"Is your brother staying long?"

"No, he's leaving tomorrow morning."

"And Euan?"

"He's been mixing with the wrong crowd, so he's staying with me for a few weeks."

"Well, I brought up two boys and both of them turned out fine, even if I do say so myself. So throw him my way if you need to."

"I may well take you up on that, and sooner rather than later. He's stroppy and uncommunicative."

Charlotte raised her eyebrows. "Sounds like normal teenage behaviour."

"You don't mean that."

"I do. Both my sons went through that phase. With Gethin it lasted until he was seventeen, and Rhys only snapped out of it when he turned nineteen."

"Great."

"Anyway, can't you remember being a teenager?"

"Just about. It was a long time ago."

Charlotte went back into the dining room. "Well, this looks like a feast." She eyed the three boxes, two of which were nearly empty. "It's not like you to eat junk food, Angus. You usually choose much healthier options. That's how you stay in such good shape." She winked at him.

Duncan picked up a box and held it out to her. "Would you like some more?"

"Thanks, but I need to get going. Lovely to meet you, Duncan." She reached out and shook his hand. "I hope we meet again soon. I've only met Angus's ex-wife, Rhona." Charlotte paused for a moment. "She doesn't like me."

Duncan looked at Angus. "Really? Why is that?"

"No idea," Charlotte stated. "I'm always pleasant to her. But I'm not losing sleep over it." She smiled.

"You keeping in touch with Rhona much, then, Ang?" Duncan asked. Charlotte stayed still, waiting for his response.

He pushed his glasses up his nose. "I've not seen her for a while."

"Well, it's nice to meet his proper family at last. I'm sure we'll be friends very quickly, Duncan. Angus always keeps things close to his chest." She gave Angus a sidelong glance, then grinned at Duncan. "You can tell me all Angus's secrets."

Chapter Nine

When Charlotte got home from Angus's, she found a note from Helena saying that she'd gone home. Helena never left notes. When this was all over, she'd have to make amends to her.

She went upstairs to check on Michelle. "Knock, knock," she called, then entered the bedroom. Michelle was lying on the bed, flicking through TV channels.

"No news?" Charlotte asked.

Michelle glanced at Charlotte. "No. I've been checking every couple of minutes. Nothing."

"Have you had something to eat?"

"I'm not hungry. How can I eat when he's god knows where, probably being tortured, or dead?"

Charlotte felt sorry for her. That irritated her. She should hate her and wish that Idris was dead too. But she just didn't have those sort of feelings. "Well, if you change your mind, let me know."

She stood there for a moment, deciding how to say what she'd discussed with Angus. In the end, she decided being forthright was best. "We need to tell the police."

Michelle turned her head towards Charlotte. "But what if they kill him?"

"We can't guarantee they haven't killed him already. We've done everything we can, and we're already running out of time."

Michelle covered her face with the palms of her hands for a few seconds. "It's only been a day. What does Angus think?"

"He agrees with me. Without access to CCTV and the police's other resources, there's not much else we can do."

Michelle sat up in bed and sighed. "Okay. The police will keep it quiet, right?"

"Of course they will. They wouldn't do anything to knowingly put someone's life at risk. I think you've made the right decision. Get dressed, and I'll call my brother."

Shortly afterwards, in the kitchen, Charlotte texted Angus to let him know what they were doing. Then she dialled her brother's number and prayed he'd pick up. Luckily, he did. "All right sis, what can I do you for?"

She took a deep breath. "Idris has been kidnapped."

Woody gave a small laugh. "You're winding me up, right? Hang on a minute, I just need to check the date's not April the first."

"I'm not winding you up, Mark. Michelle is here and we've got CCTV footage which shows him being kidnapped."

"When?"

Charlotte paused. "Yesterday," she said meekly.

"Yesterday? You'd better have a good reason for not reporting it straight away."

"Michelle begged me not to. They said they'd kill him."

There was a pause, then, "I'm surprised at you. You

should know by now that this sort of thing is best dealt with by the police."

Charlotte scoffed. "You know me … too kind for my own good."

"If the kidnapping took place at their home, you should contact the police where they live. It's not in our domain. Where did they kidnap him?"

"Hertfordshire. Haven't you got a contact over there?"

"I'm pretty sure an old buddy moved there. I'll look him up and get him to call you, or even better, Michelle. Give me her number." Charlotte gave him Michelle's mobile number and Woody ended the call. Charlotte felt a wave of relief. After a few moments she did what came instinctively: she texted Angus to come over.

It didn't take long for things to move forward. Michelle's phone rang fifteen minutes later with a blocked number. She answered and put it on speakerphone.

"Mrs Michelle Beavin?" the caller asked.

"Yes."

"I'm DCI Blake, Hertfordshire Constabulary."

Michelle breathed a sigh of relief. "Not the kidnapper," she mouthed to Charlotte.

"We've been notified by DCI Mark Lockwood at Devon and Cornwall Police that your husband has been kidnapped. Is that right?"

"Yes."

"Could we do this via video call? Then we can go through every detail."

Michelle looked at Charlotte, who nodded. "Text the link and I'll set it up."

A few minutes later, a Zoom link came through. Charlotte picked up a remote control and pressed a button. There was a soft whirring sound and a flap opened from the ceiling. A large screen, at least ten feet wide, came down.

Charlotte put the Zoom call on it just as Angus arrived. "How come I've never seen that screen before? It's the same size as the one in Piccadilly Circus."

"Ha ha. I watch films on it now and again, or use it for Zoom calls. I was thinking of converting one room into a cinema, actually. What do you think?"

Angus gave a resigned shake of his head.

She went to her computer and clicked a few buttons, and the Zoom call started. A moment later, two police officers appeared on the screen. Both wore suits and white shirts, and Charlotte thought they looked too young to be police officers. They were sitting in what looked like an interview room. Both men were slightly pixelated at first, then the picture smoothed out.

"I'm DCI Blake and this is DS Ashfield." Blake spoke with a soft Irish lilt. "Are you Mrs Beavin?"

"Not any more," said Charlotte. She moved aside and indicated Michelle, who had changed into jeans and a black T-shirt. "This is the current Mrs Beavin."

"Yes, I'm Michelle Beavin."

The Zoom call took over an hour. Charlotte sent the officers the CCTV footage and the other evidence she'd sifted through. The officers didn't comment on the fact that Michelle had hired her husband's ex-wife to find him.

"We'll send one of our family liaison officers shortly." DCI Blake shuffled the papers in front of him. "They'll keep you informed about what's going on with the investigation. In the meantime, sit tight and let us get on with finding your husband."

Michelle nodded, but when the call ended, she sat back in her chair and sobbed.

Angus pulled a handkerchief from his jacket pocket and handed it to her. "You've done the right thing. They'll be able to access all the CCTV and intelligence we can't."

"I know. I just want him back."

"Why don't you try and get some rest? You've done all you can for now... A hot bath might help too," Charlotte suggested.

Michelle nodded and went upstairs.

Charlotte turned to Angus. "They still haven't been in touch with any further information about the NFT."

Angus frowned. "I can't understand why there's been no other contact."

"It is strange."

"Is it hard to get one of these NFTs set up?"

Charlotte considered. "Not really. I can't think of any technical reason. There are plenty of places where you can mint one. Some legitimate, some not." She paused before her next words. "What are the chances of Idris being killed?"

Angus shrugged. "I don't know. I wish I could tell, but it depends how crazy these people are."

At the mention of crazy, Charlotte realised that she hadn't even thought about Misty, her therapist, since the previous morning. For once, she didn't feel as if she needed to talk to her. That was progress.

Chapter Ten

There had still been no contact from the kidnappers by the next morning. The only thing that distracted them from their frustration was Helena's arrival. She was dressed in activewear: a bralette and pink yoga leggings.

Charlotte followed her into the kitchen and they kissed each other on the cheek. "How are you, darling? Have you forgiven me yet?"

"Not yet. I been Pilates. It zo good for the mental health. You should come. It help with that horrible woman."

"I've tried Pilates, remember? I hated it. Sure, it helps your posture and it's great for flexibility, but I was so bored."

"I zink you have ADHD. You no concentrate on things."

"Getting bored easily is not the same as ADHD."

"Pilates no boring when instructor iz gorgeous man." Helena raised her eyebrows.

Charlotte couldn't suppress a smile. "Ah, so you fancy the instructor. That's why you haven't missed a class in weeks."

"He temporary. Usual instructor having baby, maternity leave for many many months. He married, but zat don't stop me looking." She beamed, then went to a cupboard and started taking out food. "Zey no find your bastard ex-husband?"

"No. Michelle is still here too."

"I know ... her car outside. You too nice."

"It's always better to take the moral high ground. Anyway, the police have been notified now. I feel as if a giant weight has been lifted."

She heard footsteps and turned. Michelle was standing in the kitchen doorway with a blank look on her face. "I should have known you'd do something like this!" she shouted. "I believed you yesterday when you said you'd do everything you could, but you just want him dead, don't you? You can't have him, so no one else can. You've just signed his death warrant." She held up her mobile phone, but the screen had gone blank.

Charlotte felt her hackles rise. "What are you talking about?"

"It's all over the news."

"What is?"

"Idris's kidnapping."

"Your screen's blank. I can't see—" But Michelle had already grabbed the remote and switched on the kitchen TV, and was scrolling through the channels.

A few moments later, Charlotte saw a thirtysomething newsreader with a serious look on her face. The scrolling text at the bottom of the screen read, "*Vipers' Nest* star Idris Beavin kidnapped."

The newsreader looked into the camera. "Little is known about the circumstances surrounding the abduction of Mr Beavin, but it is believed that he was taken a few days ago. The ransom demand is for one hundred million pounds. Tom Hunter is live outside New Scotland Yard." The shot changed to a reporter standing by the famous rotating New Scotland Yard sign.

"Wait a minute," said Charlotte. "Are you accusing me of telling the press?"

"Of course it was you," Michelle snapped. "You couldn't wait, could you? It's your revenge on us, for Idris falling in love with me and leaving you. I should have known you'd do something like this."

"Shhh, there's more..." Charlotte turned the volume up and they both listened to the news report.

"Police at Scotland Yard have confirmed that Idris Beavin has been kidnapped. No further details have been released about how he was taken. It is believed that his wife is in hiding, and Mr Beavin's friends and family are not available for comment."

"I'm not in hiding!" cried Michelle, red-faced. "You lied about me too!"

Charlotte turned the TV's volume down, wishing she could do the same to Michelle. "Look, I'm not going to argue with you. We've done enough of that. I didn't tell the press about Idris's kidnap, so you can't lay that on me. If I wanted the press to know, I would have phoned them the minute you told me."

Michelle's eyes narrowed, assessing Charlotte, then she let out a sigh. "If it wasn't you, who was it?"

Charlotte listed the names of the other people who knew, in her head: Angus, Grigore and Helena. Helena was standing on the other side of the kitchen, her back to them as she made coffee. Angus wouldn't have told them. He didn't have a reason to, and besides, he was far too principled.

Grigore was as loyal as they came. He'd never known Idris, and while he was aware of Idris's affair with Michelle, he'd never shown any emotion either way about it.

That left Helena.

"You know who it was." Michelle had always been really good at reading her face. "Angus?"

"Angus? No way!"

At the mention of his name, Angus appeared in the kitchen. Euan stood slightly behind him.

"Hello, Angus. Michelle is accusing you of telling the press about the kidnapping," Charlotte told him.

"Seriously?" Angus looked confused.

Michelle sighed. "Who, then? Who else knew? Wait – that stooge of yours. That plug-ugly bulldog who does everything you ask."

Charlotte moved towards her. "How dare you talk about Grigore like that!"

"Well, it was one of you! One of you has told the press, knowing it could get him killed."

Helena turned round. "Shut up, Michelle!" she shouted. "It vas me. I told press. I tell zem everyzing. I hate Idris and what he do to Charlotte. I no regret it." She lifted her chin. "He bastard." She spat the final words.

"Oh, Helena, you shouldn't have done that. Yes, Idris is a complete bastard, but nobody deserves to have their life put at risk just for cheating," Charlotte said.

"You too nice. I watch you heartbroken for long time, and not only for him. For *her*." She pointed an accusing finger at Michelle. "You let her stay in house. Why? She steal your husband! In Romania, none of this stupidness go on."

Everyone stared at her. "You *bitch*!" Michelle shouted.

Helena put her hands on her hips. "Takes one to know one."

"You want him dead! You actually want him dead!" Michelle glared at Helena, then ran from the room. They heard her run upstairs and a door slammed.

Helena walked to the dishwasher and started unloading it as Angus and Charlotte stood there, neither knowing what to say.

Finally, Charlotte spoke. "Helena, you shouldn't have told the press."

Helena carried on putting the clean dishes and crockery away.

"Helena, you've put his life at risk."

Helena faced her. "Have I? He still affecting your life even though you divorce. Michelle should have gone to police."

"We'll talk about it later." Charlotte knew she was dodging the issue. Helena had done it out of loyalty to her, and part of her loved Helena for it. Then she realised someone was missing. "Where's Euan?"

"Probably making himself scarce while you all argued. I'll go and find him." Angus left the room, returning shortly after. "He's in the lounge; I've put the TV on for him."

"Any ETA on the family liaison officer?" asked Charlotte.

Angus shook his head. "I can't see them being much longer, though. Couple of hours, at least, assuming there are no holdups on the A303, although from Hertfordshire, just getting around the M25 could take forever."

Charlotte checked her watch. It was nearly 10.00 am. "They can stay in a spare bedroom here if they want. Though they might want to stay in a hotel to get away from us."

"I'm sure they've arranged a hotel."

Charlotte nodded and went over to the coffee machine, grabbed a mug, slotted it in place and pressed the Americano button. When the machine had finished grinding, then brewing the coffee, she gave the mug to Angus. "Have you got something for Euan to do other than watch TV, Angus?"

"It would be good to give him something. He likes computers."

Charlotte's eyes lit up. "Excellent: a padawan of my own. I'm sure I can keep him busy with something. I could set him up on a computer with an online cybersecurity course." She got herself a coffee, then headed for the lounge. But on the way, her phone rang.

Charlotte looked at the display: Gethin. She felt a wave of sympathy for him and took the call. "Hello, my darling firstborn. I suppose you're calling because you've seen the news."

"What the hell is going on? Is it true?" Gethin's voice was anxious and strained.

Charlotte sighed. "Unfortunately, yes. Michelle is here: she's asked me to help find him. The police are involved now too."

"How could he let this happen?"

"Oh, darling, despite all his faults, he's not to blame."

"It *is* his fault. He shouldn't have gone on that stupid TV programme. It's so embarrassing."

"Really?" Charlotte was genuinely surprised.

"Why can't he just be a normal dad?"

"There's never been anything normal about your father," Charlotte said in a sarcastic tone.

"Are the police trying to find him?"

"Of course they are. Look, have you spoken to Rhys?"

"Not yet."

"I'll ring him after this call, then. Hold tight, and as soon as I hear anything, I'll let you know. I'm sure he'll be all right. As long as they haven't gagged him, they'll get fed up with his talking and let him go."

Gethin didn't laugh at his mother's joke. "Do the police know who's taken him?"

"Not yet, but I'm sure they'll find out."

"I'm really worried, Mum."

"I know. I am, too, despite everything. I'll keep you posted."

She put the phone down and called Rhys. The call went to voicemail, so she left a message. "Hello, darling. If you've seen the news about your father, try not to worry. The police are on the case. Call me when you get this."

Charlotte went to find Euan. Teaching him some cyber-security would help keep her mind off what seemed to be absolute chaos at the moment. She found him slumped on a chair, watching some programme where groups of people bid on hidden items in self-storage facilities, only discovering what was underneath the covers when they'd won the auction.

"Euan, would you like a drink?"

He shrugged.

"Come to the kitchen and I'll find you something." It was an order, not a request.

He got up slowly and loped after her. "My sons are a bit older than you, but when they were your age they loved smoothies. I have some here, I think..." She opened the fridge door and scanned the contents. "Ah yes, here we are." She pulled out a small bottle of green smoothie and handed it to Euan. "So you're staying with your Uncle Angus for a few weeks, then? How exciting. What are you going to do while you're here?"

Euan shrugged. "Angus said you can teach me to hack."

Charlotte quirked an eyebrow. "I know him well enough to know he'd never say that! However, I can teach you some computer skills, if you want to learn them. Hacking is actually quite boring and laborious. And you need permission to do it, because it's illegal."

She considered Euan. He didn't look anything like Angus. He hadn't finished growing, but there wasn't even a hint of family resemblance: Euan had a longer, more streamlined face. He was bulky and had much darker hair.

Computer skills would give Euan kudos with his friends. A friend who could hack had an almost godlike status.

"Hacking's boring?" Euan said with scepticism.

"Yep. Social engineering is much more interesting."

"What's that?"

"Manipulating people into giving you the information you need."

Euan's eyes widened, and for a moment Charlotte wondered whether she was doing the right thing. He was young and impressionable, but manipulation wasn't really something a lad his age would be capable of.

"Has your Uncle Angus brought you up to speed with what we've been working on?" she asked.

"No."

"Do you watch *Vipers' Nest?*"

She wasn't surprised when Euan shook his head. "Too busy gaming?"

"Sometimes, but I like art too."

"Well, art and computers mix. Have you done any vector graphics at school?"

Euan shook his head.

"I can show you. Anyway, my ex-husband is on *Vipers'*

Nest and he's been kidnapped. We're trying to find him." Charlotte filled in the other details of the kidnapping. "So it's all over the news now. Hopefully the police will find him."

Euan stood there, silent and awkward.

"Anyway, I hear you need something to keep yourself occupied. How about I teach you a bit of cybersecurity while we wait for the police officer to arrive?" Charlotte didn't wait for him to answer but led the way to the study.

Chapter Eleven

Charlotte had kept Euan occupied by teaching him some basic cybersecurity searches and the main internet security threats. Finally, a few hours later, the family liaison officer arrived to look after Michelle and was shown in by Helena. He was in his mid-thirties, of average height and dark haired, dressed in a dark silver-grey suit and carrying a small rucksack.

"Sorry it's taken me so long to get here: there was an RTA on the A303. I'm DC Ajay Sharma from Hertfordshire Constabulary. I've parked my car in the driveway. Is that all right?"

Charlotte stood up and shook his hand. "Charlotte Lockwood. Yes, it's fine to leave your car there. There's plenty of room. This is my colleague, Angus Darrow."

DC Sharma and Angus shook hands. "Is Mrs Beavin here?"

"Yes, she's in her room. I'll go and get her." She went to Michelle's room and knocked, but there was no response. When she entered, she found Michelle asleep.

Back downstairs, Angus had made DS Sharma a

coffee and they were sitting on the chesterfield. "Michelle's asleep," Charlotte said. "Unless you need to speak to her straight away, I think it's best to leave her for now."

"Not immediately." The police officer sipped from his mug.

"Do you have any updates on the case? Are you any closer to finding him?"

"Not yet. I had an update about an hour ago and the investigation is ongoing. They've pulled a good team together, though."

"Well, I think tracing the van via CCTV would be the best lead," said Charlotte.

DC Sharma shifted in his seat. "Er, yeah."

Charlotte sat down opposite him and sized him up. He seemed nice enough, but family liaison seemed like a waste of police time to her. "I've never quite understood what a family liaison officer does." She knew it sounded accusatory, but she felt irritable. Maybe it was because she was tired – or annoyed at Idris for allowing himself to be kidnapped. Maybe Gethin was right. If Idris hadn't plastered himself all over the TV and tried to make himself into a celebrity, they wouldn't be in this situation.

Angus spoke. "In a difficult situation like this, they act as a go-between for the police and the family. It helps aid communication, so that the family are kept up to date with everything."

"Wouldn't a phone call do?"

"No," Angus replied, giving her rather a stern look. "They're also sent to check out the family and work out if any of them are involved in the crime."

"Really?" Charlotte's eyes widened. "Well, I can tell you now that Michelle doesn't have the ability to pull off something like this." She picked up her phone and checked it.

An awkward silence fell. "So am I right in thinking that you are Idris Beavin's ex-wife?" asked DC Sharma.

Charlotte looked up from her phone. "Yep, that's right."

"When was the last time you saw your ex-husband?"

Charlotte didn't need to think. "The final negotiation with our lawyers over the divorce. That was a couple of years ago."

"What was the reason for the divorce?"

"Nosey, aren't you? He cheated on me with my best friend, Michelle. His current wife, who is upstairs." Charlotte's tone was crisp. She put her phone down and stared at DC Sharma.

"So the marriage ended acrimoniously?"

"Well, now I've discovered why you're a detective..." She turned to Angus. "Is he interviewing me?"

"Sort of," he replied. "More finding out whether you might have kidnapped Idris."

Charlotte's mouth dropped open. "Me?"

DC Sharma cleared his throat. "You're not a suspect, but it's important for any investigation that all lines of enquiry are explored."

"So you're checking me out to see if I've kidnapped my ex-husband." Charlotte's eyes narrowed. "You're just here to stick your nose in, aren't you? What possible reason would I have to kidnap him?"

"That's what he's trying to find out," said Angus. "Don't hold it against him, Charlotte. He's just doing his job."

Charlotte glared at the police officer. "Well, if he wants to find out anything else he'll have to talk to my lawyers."

DC Sharma held up a hand. "Look, I'm not here to accuse you—"

"And I won't be answering any more of your questions," Charlotte snapped. "I'll fetch Michelle. You can grill her." She stalked out of the room.

A few minutes later, Michelle came in, bleary-eyed and yawning. DC Sharma stood up and introduced himself, and Michelle gave him a wan smile. "Thank you for coming. How is the investigation going? Have they found his body yet? Now the press know he's been kidnapped, he'll probably end up dead." She glared at Charlotte.

Charlotte gave a tut that made everybody look around, but said nothing.

DC Sharma gave Michelle an update on the situation. The team in Hertfordshire were hard at work, trawling through CCTV images of the local area to try and trace the van, and looking into anyone who might have a reason to take Idris.

Charlotte pretended not to listen as she browsed on her mobile phone. The truth was that she had been racking her brain for how to help find Idris, but she had come to a dead stop. They needed that CCTV evidence, and the only way to get it was through the police.

DC Sharma and Michelle had stopped talking. "Who is in charge of the investigation?" asked Charlotte.

"DCI Ellis. I don't know him personally, but from what I hear, he is very good at his job. So you'll just have to sit tight and wait."

Charlotte nodded, though she had no idea who DCI Ellis was. She texted the name to her brother, Mark. At least there was an actual person in charge of trying to find Idris, which made her feel a bit better. But how long would this go on for?

She sent Angus a text:

Surely there's something we can do? Do we really have to sit here and let the police handle it?

Angus's phone buzzed. He looked at her, read the text, then sent a reply:

I've been trying to think of something, but I don't see what we can do. We need access to the CCTV and only the police can get it.

Charlotte replied:

I thought you were going to suggest I try and hack it :-)

That made Angus smile, and his reply came quickly.

I would never suggest you hack anything. Remember you're not supposed to tell me anything you get up to that might be even slightly breaking the rules.

Charlotte considered. Hacking the CCTV might take some time. Her best bet would be through socially engineering one of the people who worked there, or maybe a hidden virus. That would be very difficult and probably time-consuming. It was probably best just to let the police look at the CCTV themselves.

By 5.00pm Euan was starting to get bored and everyone else was moping around, so Charlotte suggested a Chinese takeaway. Afterwards, Angus and Euan left.

DC Sharma hung around until Charlotte asked him to leave for the night. If she hadn't caught him assessing whether she'd kidnapped her own ex-husband, she'd have offered him a room in her house.

Chapter Twelve

Angus spent the evening ironing, cleaning and worrying about what was going on at Charlotte's house. He had grown used to going there almost every day. He tried to remember when it had changed from an occasional thing to a habit.

He checked his emails and messages every half hour, in case there was news, then looked at the backlog of enquiries which he'd been ignoring. The background check for an old friend was done, and there were a number from people wanting to hire their services, and he thought about contacting the one at the top of the pile. But something stopped him.

Michelle turning up on Charlotte's doorstep had made him feel obliged to help out, but he was glad the police were involved now. Someone being kidnapped was bad enough, but Idris being a multimillionaire put a new edge on it. Of course the kidnappers were after his money: there was no other reason. If Idris had been the average man on the street with an average job, no way would the kidnappers have gone after him. Greed was at the heart of most crimes.

Yet something kept him from taking on further work. It was as though he had a sixth sense that he needed to keep his time free, just in case. Why, he wasn't sure.

Charlotte's initial reaction to Michelle's arrival had been milder than he'd thought. Clearly her therapy sessions with Misty were working, though he suspected she was bottling a lot of her feelings up. But that was only natural. When they'd found out that the press had got hold of the story, he'd instinctively thought Charlotte had done it. He had felt guilty once he knew it was Helena. He should have trusted Charlotte.

Angus wondered whether Idris had left money to Michelle in his will. He suspected most of it would go to the two sons, but he was certain the police would check that line of enquiry. Most likely she was better off with Idris alive, especially as it seemed he was making more money on top of the hundred million from the sale of his and Charlotte's cybersecurity company.

DC Sharma seemed to be an experienced family liaison officer. It was a difficult job, dealing with emotional and often scared family members in various situations. He'd certainly been grateful for the family liaison officers he had worked with when he was in the police. They walked a difficult line, not only dealing with their fellow officers as they investigated the crimes, but staying with family as they came to terms with it all.

It took Angus longer than usual to get to sleep, and in the early hours he heard a faint buzzing. It took him half a minute to wake up enough to realise the noise was coming from his phone. He picked it up and the display told him it was Charlotte.

"They've found Idris!" she said the moment he answered.

Chapter Thirteen

Charlotte woke. Something felt odd, then she sensed someone in the room. She lay motionless, moving her eyes rather than her head and body to look around.

In the doorway was a silhouette, sharp against the light of the hall. She blinked a few times, then realised it was Michelle and her heart stopped thumping so hard. "Is there news?"

"DC Sharma just called. They've found Idris."

"Really? Is he alive?" Charlotte sat up.

"Yes, he is!" Michelle came into the room and sat down on Charlotte's bed. "He is!" Her face was lit up by a broad smile.

"I'm really glad." And Charlotte meant it. She immediately thought of their sons, and how happy they would be. "I'll phone the boys; they're worried sick."

Michelle hugged her. "Yes. Thank you for everything. I knew we should have told the police straight away. I can't believe I didn't want to do it." She let go and jumped off the bed.

"Where is he?" asked Charlotte. "Where did they find him?"

"Near Exeter, can you believe it? They must have driven him miles. I'm not sure of anything else, but he's at the central police station now."

"Exeter?" Charlotte repeated. That was strange. He'd been kidnapped in Hertfordshire, so why had he ended up here? Surely they wouldn't have taken him this far. She didn't say anything to Michelle, but made a mental note to mention it to Angus. Maybe he'd have some idea why.

Michelle clapped her hands. "I need to get dressed and have a shower. DC Sharma offered to take me over. Idris is about to be interviewed, but they said I can see him in a couple of hours."

"I'll drive you, if you like."

"Thank you!" Michelle rushed out of the room and Charlotte picked up her phone. First to call her sons, then Angus.

"Are you going with Michelle?" Angus asked.

"Yes." Charlotte held the phone to her ear with her shoulder as she put on a pair of jeans.

"I'll meet you there."

"Are you sure? I can let you know what happens."

"I'd rather be there too."

"All right." Charlotte hadn't thought of asking Angus to come, but she was glad he would be there.

Charlotte drove them in her other car, the Volvo. They didn't speak much as she drove through the deserted streets from Topsham to the centre of Exeter.

The main police station was on Heavitree Road, not far from the city centre. It was an eyesore of 1960s' architecture. Boxy and made out of concrete, with large rectangular windows, it reminded Charlotte of her home town of

Hemel Hempstead, which had been blighted with similar buildings.

DC Sharma had already arrived and was waiting for them in the main lobby. He indicated the cheap red plastic chairs bolted to the floor. "Mr Beavin is being checked over by a doctor, and then he'll be interviewed."

Michelle frowned. "It's so stupid. Why do they need to interview him? He's been though a terrible ordeal! I want to see him."

"It isn't like that. It's more of a debrief, to find out anything we can about the kidnappers."

"Oh, I see. When can I see him? I want to see him."

"When the debrief is over, but we do need to get any information about the kidnap from your husband as soon as possible. It's vital to get as much from him as we can while it's fresh in his memory."

A few minutes later, Angus arrived, dressed in dark jeans and a plain white T-shirt. Even though those were more casual than his normal clothes, he still looked smart.

Charlotte stood up. "You didn't have to come, but I'm glad you're here."

The desk sergeant recognised him straight away. "Well, well, well. Angus Darrow. How the devil are you?" He held out his hand and Angus shook it.

"A bit tired, but it's nice to see you, Bob. How are you?"

"Oh, you know, still part of the furniture, but otherwise fine. What can I do for you?"

"I'm here about Idris Beavin. Is he all right?"

Bob nodded. "He'll be out soon, once DCI Lockwood has interviewed him. You here with them?" He indicated Charlotte, Michelle and DC Sharma.

"Yes."

Michelle went over to the desk. "How much longer?"

That made Bob straighten up. "Not long. Try not to fret, Mrs Beavin."

It was another ten minutes before Idris came out of a side room. His booming Welsh voice cut through the silence of the waiting area. "I told you I was okay, Doc. No kidnapper is gonna get the better of me."

Michelle ran towards him and he took her in his arms. "My best girl!" He wrapped her in a bear hug, lifting her off the ground.

Idris was wearing the clothes from the day of the kidnap: a black T-shirt and jeans. His sandy hair was messy and he had a considerable amount of stubble.

Angus and Charlotte stayed where they were, looking on. "He used to call me his best girl, you know," Charlotte murmured to Angus, a scowl on her face. He gave her a sympathetic look.

When Idris finally put Michelle down, she cupped his face in her hands. "Oh my darling, how are you? Was it really awful? I can't believe this even happened. I thought I'd never see you again! Did they hurt you?" She looked him up and down, assessing him.

"Just my pride," he said with a laugh. "But it takes more than a kidnapper to keep me down."

"What happened? Did someone pay the ransom?"

Idris's face darkened. "No, they just dumped me on the side of the road in the middle of nowhere. I thought they were going to kill me, but they drove off."

"My poor Iddy," she said in a babylike voice.

"Took me ages to undo the ropes on my arms and legs. When I'd done it, I walked for miles until I found a house. I knocked on the door, and they phoned the police."

"That's terrible," Michelle cooed. "When I find out who it was, I'm going to kill them. Look at your shirt – it's filthy."

"Never mind that, but I could do with a shower."

Then he saw Charlotte, and his expression changed. "Well, I never! It's Cha-Cha, my second-favourite girl! When I found out I was in Devon, I wondered if you'd stop by. Can't stop worrying about me, eh? Even though we're divorced. Come here and give me a hug."

Charlotte grimaced at the pet name he'd called her for two decades: Cha-Cha, after the dance. She'd always hated it. The last thing she wanted was a hug from Idris, but before she knew what was happening, he'd come over and picked her up in a bear hug too. He smelt as if he hadn't showered in a long time.

Michelle coughed nervously. "When I first got the demand for your ransom, I didn't know what to do. I couldn't go to the police because the kidnapper said they'd kill you if I did. So I did the next best thing. I asked Charlotte for help."

Idris put Charlotte down. "Well, I bet she wasn't much help," he said, looking into her face for a moment. "Didn't find me, did you?"

Charlotte prickled. "Don't you have an interview to go to, Idris?"

"He does," said a familiar voice in the doorway. It belonged to Woody, otherwise known as DCI Mark Lockwood, Charlotte's older brother.

Woody went to Charlotte and kissed her on the cheek, then nodded at Angus. Finally, he turned to Idris. "Idris Beavin. Long time, no see."

Idris stared up at Woody, his former brother-in-law. Woody was a good four inches taller than him, and for a moment, he looked afraid.

"I have the unenviable task of interviewing you about your kidnap, Mr Beavin."

Idris gathered himself. "Mark. How are you?" he said in a pleasant tone.

"This way, please. You can shower and change, and then we'll get to the interview."

"Can't it wait until later in the day?" Michelle piped up. "He clearly needs sleep."

"No, it can't. We need to get the info while it's fresh in his mind."

"Don't worry, I'll be out of here sooner than you think," said Idris.

Woody put a hand on Idris's shoulder and steered him through a door. DC Sharma followed.

Charlotte turned to Angus. "Is there much point in staying? How long do you think they'll be?"

"It's hard to say. A few hours, at least."

"Why don't you come back to the house in the meantime?" Charlotte asked Michelle.

Michelle shook her head. "I'm staying right here. Angus, can you sit in on the interview? That way, you'll be able to hear firsthand what happened. It might help us find out who did this."

Angus pushed his glasses up his nose. "Woody might not allow it, but there's no harm in asking. It will save Idris going over it with me at a later date, assuming you want me – us – to carry on looking into it."

Angus asked Bob to get Woody, who appeared at the door. "I can't see any reason why you shouldn't be there, Angus, as long as Idris agrees. I'll go and ask."

Moments later, he reappeared. "He says yes."

Part of Charlotte wanted to stay with Michelle, but Idris's treatment of her a minute ago had stung. "I'll go home, then. If you want to come back to my house when they let him out, you're welcome." She hadn't meant to say that, but it seemed the right thing to do. "It will save you having to find a hotel."

Michelle nodded, but looked as if her mind was elsewhere. Charlotte wasn't sure she'd even heard her.

Angus saw Charlotte to her Volvo. "Don't you find it strange that he was taken in London, yet found near Exeter?" she asked.

Angus nodded. "Yes, I do. I'll see what I can find out. Are you all right?"

"Me? I'm fine. In need of some sleep, though." She ran a hand through her hair. "The last two days have felt like an eternity. Idris was out of my life, and now he's crashed back into it in the most extraordinary way."

Angus smiled. "You've handled it really well. I'll find out everything I can and report back."

Chapter Fourteen

Angus, Idris and Woody were sat in one of the many interview rooms at the station. Angus had used room number two many times when he'd been in the police and it hadn't changed a bit. Not that there was much to change. It was a windowless room, painted light grey, with a rectangular table and three chairs.

Idris had showered, and as his clothes had been taken for forensics, he was now wearing a pair of grey sweatpants and a white T-shirt.

"Thought you'd never be inside this room again, I bet, Angus?" Woody asked, as if sensing Angus's thoughts. "Angus was a DI here for many years, Idris," he explained. "Now he works with Charlotte as a private investigator."

"So you're the bloke she works with?" Idris asked, looking Angus up and down.

"Yes."

"Slipping her one at the same time?" He gave an overexaggerated wink. "Can't say I blame you."

Angus gave Idris a piercing stare. Woody sighed. "You don't change, do you?"

"What?" Idris shrugged.

Woody shook his head a little, then pushed the button to start the recording. "Monday, May twenty-fifth, 4.09am, Exeter police station, interview with Idris Beavin, kidnap victim. Present are DCI Lockwood and Angus Darrow, who was hired by Mrs Beavin to help find her husband. He's here to observe."

Woody pulled his chair closer to the desk. Angus took out his notebook and pen. "Why don't you start from the beginning, Idris," said Woody. "Tell me about what happened when you were kidnapped."

Idris put his hand to his head. "Well, I was at home. Michelle had popped to the shops. The doorbell went, and I couldn't see who it was because they'd parked close to the door. When I opened it, a man pointed a gun at me and told me to get into the back of the van. I thought it was a joke until I realised the gun was real. They're banned and only really dodgy people have them."

"What made you think it was real?"

"I've fired a few handguns. In the US, at one of their many ranges. He shouted at me, really aggressive like, so I did what he said. He put cable ties on my wrists and shoved me into the van."

"Was anyone else in the van?"

"I didn't see anyone else, no. The back of the van was boarded up and it was pitch black, though."

"How long did he drive for?"

Idris considered for a moment. "It must have been at least half an hour. Then the van stopped, and I tried to think of a way to overcome him, but when he opened the doors we were in some kind of large garage. He shone a light on me and told me to get out. Then he must have drugged me somehow, because I can't

81

remember what happened next. I woke up tied to a chair."

"Were you in the same place?"

Idris nodded.

"Describe it."

"There wasn't much to see; it wasn't lit very well. But it was cold and big. Big enough to fit several cars in."

"And did you see the other kidnappers?"

"No. It was just him, and he wore a balaclava the whole time."

"I need you to describe him," Woody stated.

Idris shrugged with one shoulder. "He didn't take the balaclava off, so it's a bit hard. He was average height, bit stocky. Not thin, anyway."

"Age?"

"About mid-thirties, I'd say."

"What about his accent when he spoke?"

"Dunno really. All English accents sound the same to me." Idris laughed, then grew serious. "London, I think. Or near London."

Angus and Woody exchanged glances. Angus raised his eyebrows and motioned towards Idris: he wanted to ask a question. Woody nodded. "Did he talk to anyone on the phone?" Angus asked.

"Only when he phoned Michelle."

"What about messages?"

"I didn't see him text, but he might have done. I couldn't see him all the time."

"Did he leave you alone at all?"

"Only for a few minutes at a time. He got me something to eat and drink when I asked: just water and salt-and-vinegar crisps. I hate that flavour, but by the evening I was starving."

"Did he talk to you?"

"I talked to him: I wanted to find out as much as I could. But he told me to shut up and threatened to gag me. He did say there was no point in shouting because we were miles from anywhere. I listened for sounds outside – you know, cars, people, aeroplanes – but there weren't any."

Angus made notes while Woody sat with his arms folded, thinking of his next question. It didn't take him long. "So he kept you in that same place, tied up. He didn't go anywhere, and you didn't see anyone else?"

Idris nodded.

Woody exhaled. "Right. So what happened when he released you?"

"He untied my legs from the chair and told me to get in the van. I thought he was going to kill me so I thought about trying to stop him somehow, but he had the gun pointed at me the whole time. He said he'd kill Michelle if I tried anything. He drove for a long time, so long that I must have fallen asleep. Then eventually he stopped, threw me out of the van and drove off."

There was a pause as Woody and Angus considered this information.

"Did he say at any point why he took you?" asked Woody.

"No."

"Are you sure?" Woody sat back in his chair, assessing Idris.

"Of course I'm sure."

"Did he seem like a crazed fan?"

"No. He didn't mention *Vipers' Nest,* if that's what you mean."

Angus tapped his pen on the notepad a couple of times.

"Is there anything about what happened that you haven't told us? Anything at all?"

Idris thought for a moment, then shook his head. "I don't think so."

Woody stood up. "If you think of anything, contact me straight away."

"Righto."

"Have you got somewhere to stay?" Woody asked. "A hotel booked?"

"No, but I'm sure Michelle's on the case. Can't be staying at Charlotte's. That would be a bit strange, wouldn't it?" Idris laughed.

While Idris was reunited with Michelle, Angus hung back for a quiet word with Woody. "He's hiding something."

"You think so?" Woody sat back down.

"I can't put my finger on it." Angus shook his head. "Maybe I'm trying to find something that isn't there."

"The whole thing is odd. Why would they kidnap him, then set him free without collecting the ransom?"

"Cold feet?"

"Possibly."

"You've known him for years. Do you think he's hiding anything?"

Woody considered. "A few years ago, I'd have said he was an open book. But he cheated on Charlie for nearly a year and none of us knew, so anything's possible."

"What reason would he have to hide something, though?"

Woody shrugged. "I'll get my team to explore all angles. If he is hiding something, he'll regret it."

Angus's mind raced through reasons why Idris would hold information back, because he was sure he was. "Could it be that the kidnappers want him to do something for them and he has to be free to do it?"

"Like?"

"I don't know. Give them the money himself? Or facilitate some kind of deal?"

"Possibly. I'll make sure he's watched."

Angus stood up. "If I were him, I'd get some pretty tight security."

Woody headed to the door. "He's already on the case with that. I heard him on the phone earlier."

Chapter Fifteen

Charlotte didn't wake up until the afternoon, when she heard her phone buzz and forced her eyes open.

It was a text from Woody: *Idris about to do a press conference, switch on the news channel.*

Rubbing her eyes, she took the remote from her bedside table and switched the TV on. The press conference had already started, and scrolling text at the bottom of the screen stated that Idris had been found alive.

Idris was sitting behind a desk in what Charlotte presumed was a room in the Exeter police headquarters. Next to him sat a policeman in uniform. Judging by the number of stripes on his shoulder, he was a senior officer.

The police officer read from a sheet of paper. "In the early hours of last night we received a phone call from a resident on the outskirts of Exeter, informing us that Idris Beavin had been found near their property. Officers attended the scene and found Mr Beavin in the house, being cared for by the owners.

"After interviewing Mr Beavin, we established that he

had been left by the kidnappers in a country lane some distance away. He was shaken, but unharmed.

"At this time, the identities of the kidnappers are not known. However, our investigation is ongoing and we hope to apprehend them in due course. If any members of the public have information about the kidnappers, we ask them to please come forward.

"That is all the information I can give at this time. Now we will take questions."

There was a brief pause before a reporter asked, "Idris, can you tell me how you're feeling?"

Idris's stubble was gone and his hair was neatly brushed. He wore a pale-blue shirt but no tie. "I'm just relieved," he said. "I'm not going to lie: it was a horrible experience. There were times I thought I'd not get out alive, and I'm very, very glad to be free."

There was a constant clicking of cameras as Idris spoke. Charlotte could tell by the slight quaver in his voice that he was speaking from the heart. He was always a joker, looking for a laugh, but for once he was serious. Deep down, she felt a pang. It reminded her that despite their marriage being over, she still cared about him. That was annoying. She wanted to hate him, but she couldn't.

A different journalist asked, "Do you know where you were held?"

"No idea, but it was in London, I think. When they first took me, they didn't drive far."

"How did you end up in Devon, then?" another reporter asked.

"I dunno. Maybe they fancied a short break by the sea," Idris said, and laughed. Some of the reporters laughed too.

Charlotte tutted. *Always the joker.*

The police officer beside Idris spoke. "We are looking into why that was the case."

"Could it be that the kidnapper had local connections?" asked another reporter.

"We can't comment further at the moment," said the police officer.

"Was there a ransom for your safe return, and was it paid?"

"They wanted all my money, but they didn't get a penny," Idris stated.

"Do you think they got cold feet once the news broke?"

"Maybe." Idris shrugged.

"Will you have more security now?"

"Yes, but I can't discuss that in public."

"Can you tell us what happened the day you were taken?"

Idris shook his head. "I won't talk about that now. I'm saving it for my autobiography." He laughed again.

Or an exclusive with a newspaper for the right fee, thought Charlotte.

"Just one more question. Could it have been a crazed fan of yours?"

The policeman interjected before Idris could speak. "Mr Beavin can't answer any questions about who it might or might not have been. That might compromise the investigation. That's all for now."

The shot changed back to the newsroom and the main presenter sitting behind the desk.

Charlotte sat up in bed. She was pleased that Idris's ordeal was over. He looked more like his old self than he had the night before. But she wondered about his mental health: being kidnapped was no small thing. Although Idris always had a joke on the tip of his tongue, and his humour was one of the things that had attracted her to him, beneath the smiling surface he had dark moments.

Charlotte picked up her phone and checked her other messages. There was nothing from either Michelle or Idris, and she felt a small surge of anger. She'd dropped everything for them, against her better judgement, and they'd dropped her like a stone the second they didn't need her. She leaned back on her pillows and sighed. She should have known that would happen – but she had done the right thing.

After Charlotte had got dressed and had something to eat, she called Angus. She wondered why he hadn't come round, or at least texted. "Are you coming over?" she asked when he answered.

"Not yet. Why? Was there something you needed to work on?"

"It's just the fact that Idris was taken in Hertfordshire and dumped in Exeter. I thought you'd at least update me on what he said in the interview."

"I was waiting for you to contact me, to be honest. I thought you'd want to sleep in."

"That was thoughtful," Charlotte conceded. "Mark hasn't contacted me since telling me about the press conference, which means he's either too busy or ignoring me on purpose."

"He ignores you on purpose?"

"All the time."

"Really?"

"You don't believe me. Thanks."

"It's not that I don't believe you, more that you're hard to ignore."

Charlotte narrowed her eyes, though he couldn't see her. "Tell me what you know."

Angus told her what Idris had said in the interview. "So it's still a mystery as to why and who. The police are assuming for now that Idris was left near Exeter because that's where Michelle was, but they're not sure how the kidnapper knew that. Woody did say that they think it was just one person."

"That's unlikely, isn't it? Don't kidnappers work in gangs?"

"Usually, yes."

"It's all very strange. Is there no CCTV of the van? It must have been captured somewhere between London and Exeter."

"They're working on it, but no news yet. Woody has already passed a lot of info to me – too much, really. We shouldn't pressure him to bend confidentiality any further."

"It's my ex-husband, though."

"I just think we need to leave it to the police. They'll get there, and they have the resources. Plus it's a high-profile case, so they won't let it drop. I'll come over and we can discuss what to do next. Is it still okay to bring Euan?"

"Yes, bring him over. Teaching him some more cyberse-curity will distract me."

When Angus pulled up outside Charlotte's house, he was surprised to see another car in the driveway which he recog-nised straight away. It belonged to his old sergeant, Simon Pearce.

Simon was just getting out of the car, and Angus raised a hand in greeting. "Simon, it's good to see you."

"Sir! I mean, Angus. How are you? I wasn't expecting to

see you here." Simon walked over and offered his hand, and Angus shook it.

Euan got out of the passenger side and closed the door. He stood awkwardly, hands in pockets and hood up.

"Good, thank you. Is there a reason you're here?"

"I need to talk to Charlotte Lockwood. This is her house, isn't it?"

"It is. I take it this is about the kidnapping?"

Simon nodded, then leaned in and lowered his voice. "The powers that be have asked me to look into her to see whether she might be responsible for kidnapping Idris Beavin. He's her ex, right?"

"Yes, he is." Angus suppressed his surprise, then felt a sudden irritation. "Does Woody know?"

"Yeah, and he blew a gasket about it. Between you and me, he might get taken off the case: he's too close to it. Obviously the higher-ups don't think Charlotte did it herself, but she could have hired someone."

"Motive?" Angus fired back, annoyed at his former sergeant.

Simon shrugged. "Payback? He cheated on her with her best friend, after all. They're going to check her finances, and I get to talk to her."

"Wait – how did you know he cheated on her?"

Simon had started to walk up the drive, but stopped at Angus's question. "I heard it on the grapevine a while ago. Woody confirmed it when someone asked if it was true."

Angus thought about the strength of character that Charlotte had shown while she tried to get over what had happened. He knew her well enough to know that she'd never do something like orchestrate a kidnapping. She was kind and compassionate, and she'd never knowingly hurt anyone, however much they hurt her. He put his hands in his pockets. "You're barking up the wrong tree, Simon."

Simon shrugged again. "I have to follow it up. It's just a few questions. You know how it is."

"I'll go and get her." *Warn her, more like.*

Angus went up the drive, followed by Euan. Helena let him in, and he sent Euan to the study, leaving Simon to introduce himself to Helena. Then he went upstairs to find Charlotte. He'd never actually been upstairs at Charlotte's house. He'd wondered what it was like, but had never asked.

At the top of the stairs he had the choice of what seemed liked dozens of doors, all slightly open. Instead of knocking, he called, "Charlotte?"

There was a creak from the second room on the left. A moment later, Charlotte peeped around the door. "Hello." She smiled and opened the door a little more.

This was going to be difficult. What he was about to tell her would wipe the smile from her face in an instant. He pushed his glasses up his nose. "My old sergeant is downstairs. He wants to talk to you about Idris's kidnapping."

She blinked twice. That was never a good sign. Then her eyes narrowed. "Why?"

"They're looking into whether you were behind it all."

"He thinks I arranged Idris's kidnapping?" She snorted, then came onto the landing. She was wearing a long dark-green skirt and a cream shirt. Angus looked past her for a moment and saw what must be her bedroom. A huge four-poster bed covered by a white bedspread contrasted with the dark-green walls.

"They're seriously looking into me?" she said quietly.

"I don't think it's serious. I'm guessing they want to tick the box and eliminate you from the investigation."

Her eyes narrowed even further. "Does Mark know?"

"Yes, and he isn't happy about it. Look, you can talk to the guy if you like. He's my old sergeant, Simon, and a good man."

Charlotte went back into her room and returned a moment later with her phone. "I'm not talking to anyone without my lawyer. This is ridiculous. Are they really so desperate that they think I did this?"

"Woody isn't, but he knows you. The thing is, you do have a motive"—he held his hands up as she scoffed—"but they have to cover all angles."

Charlotte walked past Angus and downstairs to the living room. Angus wasn't sure what she was going to do, but he followed her.

Chapter Sixteen

Charlotte eyed the man in front of her. "And you are?" she asked, in her most patronising tone.

"DS Simon Pearce." He held his hand out. Charlotte looked at it, then at his face, but didn't take his offered hand. The officer moved his arm back and gave her an awkward smile.

"You want to talk to me about my ex-husband?" she asked, in the same tone.

"I do. It's just a few routine questions."

"Well, unless I'm under arrest, I don't have to talk to you. My lawyer is on his way, and after I've spoken to him, he'll be in contact. Leave your card on the table, please. Goodbye." She walked to a table and pressed a button in its side.

DS Pearce stood there, staring at her. "Er, are you sure you don't want to talk to me?"

"I'm absolutely sure, thank you."

Simon looked at Angus, who stood silent. "Okay." He took a card from his back pocket and put it on the table.

Grigore appeared at the door. "Ah, Grigore," said Charlotte. "See the police officer out, please."

When Charlotte heard the front door close, she turned to Angus. "I'm sorry if this affects your friendship with your old sergeant."

"He's not my friend, he's an ex-colleague."

She nodded. "Tell him it's nothing personal."

She touched the screen on her phone, then walked to the window. "David, I need you to deal with the police... Yes, the police... They want to talk to me about Idris's kidnapping. They're checking I'm not behind it. No, of course it isn't my brother. He knows I'd never do something so awful. I'll send the details. Thanks, okay, bye."

She turned back to Angus. "My lawyer will deal with him." She sat down on the nearest chair and ran her hands through her hair. "This is getting so complicated. I really wish I knew who's behind this, because it's a nightmare from start to finish. I'm not supposed to have all this stress. What will Misty say?"

"She'll say you're handling it really well. Because you are." Angus sat next to her.

Charlotte nudged his arm with hers. "You always say the nicest things."

"I just speak the truth. Look, why don't you spend some time teaching Euan? It will take your mind off things, and he really enjoyed the stuff you did before."

Charlotte's face softened. "All right."

Charlotte was teaching Euan in her study when her phone rang. She glanced at the time: five o'clock. The display said *Michelle*.

"Euan, why don't you go and get a snack from the kitchen while I take this call?"

Euan nodded and got up.

She picked up the call. "Are you finally calling to thank me for helping?"

Angus was working on his accounts on the other side of the room. He glanced up, then looked down again.

"No, I'm not," Michelle snapped. "Your brother has brought Idris back in for more questioning."

"Oh. From the sound of your voice, that's a bad thing?"

"He's accusing Idris of setting up his own kidnap."

It took Charlotte a moment to process this information. So the police had moved on from looking into her to suspecting Idris himself? That was both ironic and rather pleasing. "I don't believe for a minute that Idris set up the kidnapping himself," she said, for Angus's benefit.

"I know, right? I can't believe your brother actually thinks that."

"Mark must have a reason for thinking it, though," said Charlotte. "Something can't be right, or they wouldn't even consider it."

"Trust you to take your brother's side," Michelle muttered.

"I'm not! They're investigating me, too, you know. And they're probably checking you out. They're just covering all angles. He's not under arrest, is he?"

"No, they're just questioning him. His lawyer is with him."

"Well, that's all right, then. I'm sure he's got a decent one. And, as he didn't do it, he's got nothing to worry about."

"But—"

"Sorry, got to go." Charlotte ended the call before

Michelle could say anything else. She put her phone on the table and sighed.

Angus folded his arms. "Are you sure he isn't behind it?"

"Absolutely. He's done some stupid things in his time, but even he's not stupid enough to do that!"

Angus said nothing.

Charlotte raised her eyebrows. "You think he might be?"

"I don't know," Angus replied. "In the interview I got the feeling that he was hiding something."

"Like what?"

"I don't know."

"Well, that's no help."

"And there's also the fact that they let him go, close to where Michelle was, and despite asking for a huge ransom, they didn't follow through."

Charlotte stood up and stretched. "Michelle didn't have a clue, though. She was frantic."

"I agree. There's no way she was acting."

"*If* he did it, what motive would there be? He hasn't lost any money, according to Michelle."

Angus thought. "He likes the limelight; maybe it was a publicity stunt. There was that case in America where an actor faked an attack on himself."

"I remember that. The judge said he craved attention." Idris had always been the life and soul of the party, who loved making people laugh. But doing something outlandish just to get in the news? She shook her head. "I can't see him doing something so stupid, and he'd never waste police time. What was he like in the interview? Did he seem like he was acting?"

"No. And your brother seemed to think it was real."

"So we're back to square one. It's all just a hot mess. Until the police can work out who was behind it, they're pointing the finger at everyone."

"They have to explore all possibilities," said Angus.

Charlotte huffed. "Yes, but then they should move on to the actual culprits."

"They're trying, but they've drawn a blank."

"We need to move on to another case," said Charlotte. "I need a distraction. If the police can't work out who it was, and we've tried and failed, I don't know what to do."

Angus raised his eyebrows. "You don't normally give up so easily."

She sighed. "For anyone other than Idris, I wouldn't. But dealing with all this has been hard, and though I've been trying to move on, it's stalled my recovery." She pressed her palm to her forehead. "God, I don't mean to make it all about me, really I don't. I wasn't kidnapped, and for that I'm grateful, but it's affected me too. That's all." She looked up at Angus and smiled. "So, what other cases have we got lined up?"

Angus took out his phone and pulled up an email. "I've had an interesting request from someone today actually. They've asked me to trace someone who used to live in their house in the sixties."

Charlotte studied him and saw a flash of something in his eyes. Passion? Enthusiasm? "Why do they want to do that?"

"They found a tin full of old photos in their attic. They look as if they have sentimental value."

"And you're interested because...?"

"I like historical cases. You know, ones that mean something. And he's prepared to pay a lot of money."

"Everyone has their price." Charlotte smiled.

"The extra money will go towards the deposit on my next property investment."

"Are you trying to be the next Donald Trump?"

He chuckled. "No, I'm not."

"All right, let's give it a go. It's certainly different. And isn't a change as good as a rest?"

"I'll call him."

Chapter Seventeen

"Thank you for getting in touch with me so quickly," said Oliver Trent. "I'm so grateful to you for agreeing to come and see me." He was in his mid-thirties, with sandy hair, dressed in smart jeans and a shirt.

They were standing in a large, white, modern kitchen. The building was an old farmhouse on the edge of the Exeter side of Dartmoor. But despite being old, it was modern and fresh inside. A lot of money had clearly been spent on doing it up. It was like a show home, bare and minimalist.

"I haven't owned this property long," said Oliver. "Just a few months. It's my second home: a bolt-hole from the hectic London life. I know that won't make me very popular with the locals, but I do intend to live here full-time in a year or so." He smiled at Charlotte. "Coffee?"

Charlotte shook her head, but Angus nodded. "Thank you."

He went to the cupboard, looked inside, then tried the next one. "Ah, there they are. Always misplacing them."

He took out a coffee pod and placed it in the nearby machine.

When the coffee was made, they went into the lounge. It was as minimal as the kitchen. Light-grey walls and a dark wooden floor, with a pale-grey tartan rug covering most of it. The chairs and settee were light grey, too, and looked almost new. In the middle of the room was a coffee table with a vase of spring flowers on it.

Angus and Charlotte sat next to each other on the sofa and Oliver stood by the window. He looked out onto the drive. "Is that your car and driver out there?" He indicated Grigore, who was smoking a cigarette beside the Bentley. "And the other car is yours, Mr Darrow?"

"The Bentley's mine, yes," said Charlotte. "So, how can we help you?"

Oliver stared at Grigore a moment longer, then sat down. "Well, when I bought the property, they left a few items in the attic, and I found this." He reached for a tin box on a nearby table. "Inside are lots of photos. Although most of them are fairly ordinary – trips to the seaside, that sort of thing – some have people's names on the back. One has a list of their names, and the woman in the middle is listed as a 'most beloved mother'."

"Wouldn't you be better posting it on a family-history website?" said Charlotte. "There are several of those. Or maybe Facebook pages for the area. There are plenty, you know."

Oliver stared at Charlotte, then gave her a small smile. "I've tried that, but to no avail."

"It's very noble of you, but they're just photos," she replied. "Why would you worry about returning them?" Something about Oliver was getting to her: he barely took his eyes off her. Her chest felt tight and her shoulders were tensed up. She didn't feel like massaging his feelings by being nice.

Oliver pondered for a moment. "I suppose I'm being sentimental. I lost my own mother a few years ago, you see. I thought the person who wrote this might still be alive and want the photos back. The previous owners only had it a few years, so it's not theirs. Beyond that, I had a quick look but couldn't find out who owned it before that." He paused again. "I know it's eccentric, but I have all this money, and half the time I don't know what to do with it."

Charlotte glanced at Angus, whose face was expressionless. She knew that look. He was concentrating on Oliver Trent.

Angus took the tin from Oliver, took out some photos and handed them to Charlotte. They were just as Oliver had said: old photos taken in what looked like the fifties and sixties. Some were black and white, others in colour.

When they'd reached the bottom of the tin, Oliver stood up and looked out at Grigore again. Then he looked at Charlotte. "Are you sure I can't tempt you with a coffee?"

"No, thanks."

Angus was about to take a sip of his drink, but Charlotte put a hand on his arm. "We need to go, Angus. We've got that other appointment." She gave him a meaningful look and stood up.

Oliver Trent looked rather surprised. "Oh. Well, I'll transfer the deposit to you straight away, and you can get to work."

When they got outside, Charlotte stopped at Angus's car. "Are you buying this?" She leant against the driver's door so he couldn't get in.

"What do you mean?"

"Don't you think it's a bit strange that he wants us to find the owner of the photos?"

Angus pursed his lips, thinking. "Not really. I know how eccentric the super-rich can be."

"What's that supposed to mean?" Her eyes narrowed. "I'm not eccentric."

He smiled. "Rather arrogant that you think I'm talking about you, Charlotte."

"Who else do you know who's super-rich?"

"Your ex-husband, for a start."

"You've only met him briefly. You don't really know him."

Angus shrugged. "Look, this is a different case to the usual. It isn't a kidnapping, or a spouse wanting their partner followed. So I'm going to take it."

Charlotte moved away from the car. "Fine, take the case, but the easiest way to find out is to use the internet. You'll want me to look things up, and my heart isn't in it."

"I could start Euan on it first... Anyway, what don't you like about him?"

"I don't dislike him. I don't know him."

Angus raised his eyebrows.

Charlotte leant against his car again. "Look, he gave me the creeps. You wouldn't understand: it's a female thing. He wouldn't stop staring at me. It was almost as though you weren't in the room. And he kept asking me if I wanted a coffee. I learnt years ago never to trust a man who keeps trying to get you to drink something."

"I did notice that he kept looking at you," said Angus. "Lots of men look at you, though. You're an attractive woman."

Charlotte tilted her head, studying him. "So you think I'm attractive?"

Angus blushed. "Yes ... no ... I mean yes, you are. He's no different to plenty of other men we've met."

There was an awkward silence. Charlotte felt a glimmer of hope at his confused words. Then it was extinguished by the thought of Oliver. "Right," she said briskly. "You try and find out as much as you can to trace this person, and if you and Euan get stuck, I'll help. Just like I always do." She walked towards the Bentley, Grigore opened the door and she got in.

"You go home?" Grigore asked, when he was settled in the driver's seat.

"No, I need to go into Exeter and get a few things. Drop me off near the cathedral." Anything to kill time, because if she went straight home, she knew she'd end up helping Angus, even though he hadn't asked.

As Grigore drove, Charlotte fumed. Why Angus was taking on this case was beyond her. Was it just the money? Maybe he was getting more mercenary. Maybe he'd always been mercenary and she hadn't noticed.

No, that wasn't fair. Of course Angus wanted to make a living: he was planning another flat conversion, and he needed money for that. Either way, he would need her help at some point in the case.

And yet they hadn't argued like this before, though they had undertaken plenty of boring, predictable investigations. So why was she touchy with him now? Maybe, she admitted to herself, it was because she was getting fed up with the fact that he didn't feel the way about her that *she* felt about him.

She needed to talk to Misty. Misty would tell her exactly what to do – which would, most likely, be absolutely nothing. Either that, or find another man, start dating and get out there again.

The thought of going out on dates filled her with dread and fear. When she'd been sleeping with any man who took her fancy, it meant nothing. It hadn't fulfilled her: it had been a reaction to her divorce.

Then there was the fact that she was a multimillionaire. How would she know a man was interested in her, and not her money?

Some of her friends used dating apps, and they sat swiping through men's profiles, judging them on a photo and a few words. She didn't like the idea of men doing that to her. It was all so shallow. She preferred the old-fashioned way – meeting someone in real life.

Things had been much easier before the internet, when you had to talk to men before dating them.

No. Dating apps were a no-no, forever.

In Exeter, Charlotte went from shop to shop, but nothing excited her, not even the eclectic independent shops on Fore Street.

She made her way back up to the high street and stood at the junction of North Street and High Street, waiting for the green man at the pedestrian crossing. A number of other people were standing nearby, waiting to cross or chatting.

Charlotte continued to wait, growing impatient. Surely the lights would change soon. Then a car was about to go past, and she was shoved from behind and stumbled into its path.

Chapter Eighteen

A woman standing next to her was also pushed into the passing car, but Charlotte bore the brunt of it. A sharp pain shot through her leg and she cried out.

The next thing she knew, she was lying on the cold pavement with a crowd around her. A man, most likely the driver, was shouting, "The lights were green; I just heard a thump. Are you all right, love?"

"Of course she isn't all right. You hit her with your car!" said an onlooker.

"Someone call an ambulance," a woman said.

"Can you stand up?" another man asked.

Charlotte tried to move her leg. The sharp pain came again, just below the knee, and she yelped.

It seemed to take an age for the ambulance to arrive. When it did, she was almost passing out from pain.

The next few hours were a blur. Doctors, nurses, an IV, X-rays, sensors, clips and electrodes attached to her, and questions about her and her next of kin.

Fiona, her sister-in-law, took time out from her nursing

duties to come and see her. "Oh my goodness, what happened?" She took her hand and Charlotte instantly felt better.

"Car vs woman. Car won," Charlotte muttered.

She asked Fiona to contact Helena, but by the time Helena arrived she was too groggy with drugs to know much. She woke up in the early morning with a faint memory of Helena having visited and terrible pain in her leg, and begged the nurse for more pain relief.

By 9.00am, Fiona was back, and this time Charlotte was more lucid. "Mark came last night: he was worried sick. You were asleep, so you won't know."

"Mark?"

"He's at work now, trying to find out what happened. Do you remember anything?"

Charlotte shook her head. "Am I going to be all right?"

"Yes, thankfully. You've got a fracture on your left leg and they're going to operate this morning. They'll put some pins in, and you'll be in a cast for six to eight weeks. You'll need lots of physiotherapy, but nothing else was damaged. I think you were in shock. You'll be able to go home in a few days."

"I haven't felt pain like that since giving birth," Charlotte croaked. She laid her head on her pillows and sighed. "I'd better rejoin Netflix. I'll have a lot of spare time to watch TV."

Fiona kissed her on the head. "Helena, Grigore and Angus are champing at the bit to see you, but it's better they stay away until you're out of surgery. The surgeon will be here soon to go through everything with you, and you'll have to sign for permission. Then the porter will come and take you down shortly." Fiona squeezed her hand. "I've got to go, but they've promised me I can be with you when you go to theatre."

Angus had been at home with Euan, looking into the new case, when Grigore rang. At first he hadn't even realised that it was Grigore. He was crying, and his Romanian accent was even thicker than normal.

"Slow down and repeat what you said, Grigore. Did you say that Charlotte has been hurt?"

"Yez. She hit by car in Exeter. It all my fault."

"Wait – is she okay?"

"She in hospital."

"But she's alive, yes?"

"I don't know!" he sobbed.

"Grigore, were you with Charlotte when it happened?"

"No, that why it my fault! I no protect her!" Grigore sobbed harder than before, and Angus realised he wouldn't get any more out of him.

Angus rang Helena, but she didn't answer the phone, which worried him even more. Then he tried Woody and got his voicemail.

He tried to think who else he could ring, but drew a blank. He told himself that, of course, Charlotte would be fine. *But what if she isn't? What would I do without her?*

He wouldn't allow himself to think the worst, but if she was hurt badly...

He'd got used to Charlotte. They worked together well, and the more he got to know her, the more he liked her. While she could be excruciatingly annoying at times, she also brought a light into his life that hadn't been there since – well, since he had last been in love. But that had been decades ago, with Rhona, his ex-wife.

And yet—

Suddenly Angus felt as if someone had lit a small fire inside him. *Don't be ridiculous*, he told himself.

"What's going on?" asked Euan. "What was that phone call about?"

"It's Charlotte. She's been hit by a car." Angus's heart sank at having to say it out loud.

Euan's mouth opened slightly. "Is she going to be okay?"

Angus took a deep breath. "I don't know."

"You could go to the hospital and find out," Euan suggested.

"I think I will." Angus stood up to find his car keys, and his phone rang.

It was Woody. "Sorry, mate, I was busy with stuff, as you can imagine, and I missed your message. Charlie's going to be all right. She's broken her leg and they need to stick a few pins in it, but there are no other injuries. Fiona is with her."

"Can I visit her?"

"Not yet. Surgery is in the morning and she's drugged up because of the pain. I'll keep you posted as much as I can. Just sit tight and she'll be back soon enough, annoying the hell out of us. But I tell you what, if I find out there's someone behind this... Gotta go now. I'll call you when I have more news." And he rang off.

The relief Angus felt was indescribable. He sat motionless for a few moments, taking in the news. *She's going to be all right.*

Euan walked in. "Is she okay?"

Angus put his phone on the table. "She's broken her leg, and she'll be in hospital for a few days, but otherwise, yes."

Euan put his hands in his pockets. "That's a shame about her leg. She's been teaching me loads."

"Well, you can help by giving me a hand with the photos. Show Charlotte that you can apply what she's taught you. Find out anything, even if you think it's insignificant."

"All right." Euan left the room.

Angus sighed and looked out of the window at nothing in particular. At least that would keep Euan busy.

The next morning, Angus almost jumped out of his skin when his phone rang. He grabbed it, and saw that the caller was Oliver Trent. "Hello," he said abruptly.

"Mr Darrow, so sorry to bother you, but I have some good news. Well, it's good news for me, though not so much for you."

"Go on."

"Someone local who knows the family saw the photos on a website I posted them on, and they've put me in touch with them now. I'm so sorry to have wasted your time. I'll pay you for the time you've taken and a little extra for troubling you. I am so grateful to you for prioritising my case. Will you also thank your lovely colleague, Miss Lockwood?"

"Well, thank you for letting me know, Mr Trent. I'll send you my bill."

"I'll pay it as soon as I receive it. Many thanks, Mr Darrow."

Being off that case was a relief. Since the news about Charlotte, Angus had found it hard to concentrate, which was unlike him. Normally work distracted him from stressing about things.

Angus considered the other enquiries he had received lately. What could he take on? More possible insurance fraud, or one of the string of suspicious spouses. He'd leave it for a few days, though, and concentrate on Euan. He'd take him to some interesting places in Devon. That would distract them both.

He went to find Euan and tell him the plan. Unsurprisingly, he was in his room, staring at the screen of the laptop Charlotte had lent him.

Angus sat down on the bed. "We don't need to find the owner of the photos any more, Euan. Mr Trent just called to say he's been put in touch with them."

"Who was it in the end?" asked Euan, looking up from the laptop.

"I didn't ask, and he didn't say." That was unlike him. He couldn't believe that he hadn't asked. *I'm losing the plot.*

Angus began to stand up, then saw that Euan had TikTok open. "Now, Euan, what did your dad say? No social media while you're here."

Euan assumed a hurt expression. "It isn't for fun. I've been searching all the major sites for photos or videos of Charlotte's accident."

Angus frowned. "Why are you doing that? What makes you think there would be any?"

Euan shrugged. "No one walks out in front of a car, do they? I figured that if there was a video or something, it would help Charlotte if she wanted to sue the driver."

"And did you find anything?"

"Sort of. A couple of students in Exeter filmed themselves on TikTok, and you can see some of it." Euan turned the laptop to face Angus and pressed play.

It showed a video with the text label, "Uh-oh, accident!" People were running to a small group bending over someone on the pavement. The person was hidden, but it was the High Street. The camera moved closer to the crowd and a caption came up: "Hope she's all right." Then the video began again. Angus watched it through, then frowned as the camera moved closer. He recognised Charlotte's clothes. "Can you pause it?"

Euan hit the space bar. "Have you seen something?"

"Might have." Angus peered past the caption at the bystanders. One wore jeans and a familiar shirt, and had sandy hair. The camera had captured his profile.

Oliver Trent. What was he doing there?

"Well done, Euan." Angus put a hand on his shoulder. "Good work."

Chapter Nineteen

Angus called Woody straight away. "I have a lead for you on Charlotte's accident." He told him what they'd found.

"Oliver Trent might just have been in Exeter," said Woody.

"When we'd met with him immediately beforehand? That's too much of a coincidence. And he couldn't stop looking at Charlotte when we were at his house. She said when she left that she had a bad feeling about him." Angus's mouth twisted as he remembered something. "Besides, he phoned me earlier and told me to thank Charlotte for her help. He didn't mention her accident."

"Maybe he didn't see it was her."

"Unlikely, given that he was right there."

"What do you want me to do, Angus?"

"I want you to look into him."

"Send his details over and I'll take a look."

"Thanks. Have you any more news of Charlotte?"

"She's in surgery. I'll text you when I know more."

Angus went straight back to Euan. "I want you to find

out as much as you can about Oliver Trent. I need everything you can find, no matter how small or insignificant. Find out his inside leg measurement if you can."

Euan stared at him. "Really?"

Angus sighed. "That bit was a joke."

Euan took the notepad. "Do you think he had something to do with Charlotte's accident?"

"I don't know, but I do want to know what he was doing there, and why he didn't mention it when I spoke to him this morning."

Euan nodded and set to work.

"Is that comfortable, Charlotte?" Fiona smoothed the pillows she had just finished adjusting.

Charlotte nodded. Her head was still swimming after the operation, but she was glad to be home. It was only because Fiona had arranged for private nurses to come and look after her that she had been allowed out of the hospital so soon. "I'd be more comfortable if I didn't have this horrible hospital gown on, though."

Fiona smiled. "I'll get the nurse and we'll put you in one of your own nightshirts. Try and rest for now, though. The anaesthetic will take some time to fully leave your system."

Charlotte must have fallen asleep, because it was dark when she woke again. A nurse sat in the corner of the room. She didn't recognise her, but she was too weak and dazed to do anything about it.

When she woke again, it was morning. She checked her phone: 9.36am. She felt groggy. There was no nurse in the corner now, but a wireless bell had appeared, so she pushed it.

A moment later, a woman came in wearing nurse's

scrubs and a name badge. Her slightly greying brown hair was in a neat ponytail. "Good morning, Miss Lockwood. I'm Jen and I'm your nurse today."

"Any chance of some painkillers?" Charlotte murmured.

"Absolutely. I've been waiting for you to wake up so that I can give you some more. I need to check your vitals first, though."

Next to her bed was an array of medical equipment. Jen picked up a blood-pressure monitor and secured the cuff around Charlotte's arm. It squeezed so tight that it hurt, then just as she thought it couldn't get any tighter, it eased off.

"How long will I need nursing?"

"Just a couple of days. You're popular," Jen commented. "There's a queue of people waiting to see you."

"Who?"

"Grigore and Helena have been flitting about. I thought you were being burgled this morning when I heard someone coming in."

"They come and go as they please. They don't live here, but they sometimes sleep in one of the spare rooms."

Jen put the blood-pressure monitor back and wrote the reading in the notes. "Blood pressure is fine. Your sister-in-law, Fiona, is lovely. I met her back in the day when I started training. She was my staff nurse for a while."

"She's the best." Charlotte tried to sit up, but the cast on her left leg stopped her. She pushed the bedcovers aside and looked at it. Her toes poked out at the bottom and it went up to her knee.

A few hours later, Charlotte was dozing, having eaten, drunk and taken some painkillers the size of horse pills, which worked wonders. She struggled out of unconsciousness as she heard voices at her bedroom door. Jen was there, blocking someone from coming in. "She's asleep."

"I need to speak to her."

I know that voice. Charlotte smiled. "Angus?"

That made Jen move back, and Angus went to her bedside.

"Why are there two of you?" Charlotte giggled. That was some good luck, two Anguses.

Angus crouched down beside her. "Hello, there. I've been worried about you."

"Both of you?" She smiled.

Jen moved behind Angus. "She's on some powerful painkillers, so you might not get much out of her."

"Charlotte, I need you to tell me everything you can about what happened when the car hit you."

"Car..." she repeated.

"Yes. Can you remember what happened?"

"Car hit me. Car won."

"What else?"

Charlotte closed her eyes and tried to concentrate, but there was nothing. "I can't remember."

"It's probably the painkillers," said Jen. "She'll remember more when she can come off them."

"When will that be?" Angus asked.

"We're reducing the dose every time, and then we'll swap to something less addictive which she'll take for a month or so. She's had a big operation, you know. It's best you leave her to sleep."

Angus sighed and stood up. "Okay, thanks."

Downstairs, Angus found a subdued Helena in the kitchen, stirring something in a large saucepan. "I make special

Romanian chicken soup for her. It called ciorba radauteana."

"It smells delicious."

"Of course. Usually in Romania we eat it if we have cold or flu." She shrugged. "But I figure it help her now too."

Angus grew serious. "Helena, I need your help. Euan has been looking into a former client of ours. We saw him the day Charlotte was hit by the car."

"And?" Helena shrugged, then took a bowl out of the cupboard and ladled some soup into it.

"Euan couldn't find out anything about him. Despite it being a fairly common name, he's looked into everyone with the same name and he doesn't exist. The property that he said was his is an Airbnb. He found the listing."

"Why he lie?"

"I don't know. But all the time we were there, he couldn't take his eyes off Charlotte. She said he gave her the creeps."

Helena frowned, then gave Angus the bowl and a spoon. "Try."

"Thanks. Euan also found a TikTok filmed just after Charlotte's accident, at the scene. He was close by when Charlotte got hit."

"Zat's suspicious."

"Yep."

"People film and put on social media someone hit by car. Zat sick."

"Yes. But I'm starting to worry that Charlotte is in danger."

"Really?"

"Yes. I might be wrong, but until I'm sure, you need to keep a close eye on her. Can you stay here at night? And Grigore too?"

"Of course. Have you sent photo to Mark? They have face scanners, no?"

"Facial recognition. Yes, I did that, but he isn't in the police database so there's not much we can do. He used a fake ID and a stolen credit card."

Angus took out his phone, pressed the screen a few times, and showed Helena the photo of the man who called himself Oliver Trent. "Do you recognise him?"

Helena looked at the photo. "No, never seen him before."

"Charlotte had never seen him before either. Can you think of anyone who might want to hurt her?"

"No."

Angus tried the soup; it was delicious. "Does anyone in Charlotte's past bear a grudge towards her?"

"I don't zink so. She always lovely to everyone."

"When she's a bit more coherent, can you speak to her and see if she can think of anyone. Write down anyone she mentions, even if she thinks there's not much chance. Let me know when you have that list."

Helena nodded as Grigore entered the kitchen. "You vant soup?" she asked him. "I make plenty."

Grigore nodded, but at Angus rather than Helena, in a silent acknowledgement of their phone call a few days before.

"I'm glad you're both here. I want you to get proper protection for Charlotte." Grigore moved forwards as if to say that he was the protection. "I know you'll do everything you can to look after her, Grigore, but I mean armed protection. Can you sort it?"

"You really zink she at risk?" said Helena, the ladle poised over the pan. "You zink the car thing vas on purpose?"

"I'm not sure," said Angus, "but until we find out, I want every precaution to be taken."

Helena shook her head. "I don't know ver to find armed guard."

"She must have some millionaire or billionaire friends with guards."

"Ross," Grigore grunted over his bowl of soup.

Helena nodded. "Yez, Ross he know. He her ... friend with benefits." Helena giggled.

Angus felt a stab of jealousy. "All right. Tell him you need the information A-S-A-P. Grigore, until the guard arrives, don't let anyone in this house, other than the nurses, the three of us, or Fiona and Mark. Dial nine-nine-nine and ask for the police if there's anything suspicious. I'll update Woody."

Grigore nodded.

Angus left the kitchen. His mind was in a whirl, but he felt exhilarated. It seemed like an age since he'd left the police, and he hadn't realised until that moment how much he'd missed having a crisis to deal with. He'd rather Charlotte hadn't been the one at risk, though. He just hoped the protection would get there quickly. Once he had a list of possible suspects from Charlotte and Helena, he'd start looking into them. Of course, he could be completely wrong, and it might just have been an accident, but the fact that Oliver Trent apparently didn't exist reminded him that something wasn't right.

He went into Charlotte's office and dialled Idris's phone number.

Idris answered quickly. "All right, Angus, you been able to find out who was behind my kidnapping yet?"

Angus felt himself tense up. "I need to talk to you in person. Where are you?"

"Why?"

"You've heard about Charlotte, I take it?"

"No, what's happened?"

"She was hit by a car."

There was a long pause. "That's terrible. Is she okay?"

"She will be. Are you still near Exeter? I need to talk to you."

"I'm in Wales, at my farmhouse. It's where I go to get away from everything."

"Give me the address, and I'll be there as soon as I can."

Chapter Twenty

It took Angus nearly three hours to drive to Idris's place in Wales. The M5 section was quick, but the property was in the sticks, and the winding rural roads seemed to go on forever.

When he pulled up outside the farmhouse's metal gates, he pressed the buzzer.

"Yeah?" said a voice from the speaker.

"Angus Darrow to see Idris Beavin."

"Drive through and park in front of the house." The gates slowly opened and Angus drove on.

A long, winding road led to the Tudor-style farmhouse. He parked close to it and turned off the engine.

A burly man with an earpiece, dressed in black and holding a handheld metal detector, stood by the main entrance. "You Angus Darrow?" he said in a flat voice when Angus got out.

Angus nodded.

"Got some ID?"

Angus took out his wallet and found his driver's licence.

The man looked at it, then handed it back. "Arms up, please."

Angus obliged and the man waved the detector around him. "Come with me."

The farmhouse was immaculate inside. Angus had expected nothing else. The original wooden beams had been painted black, contrasting with the white walls. Everything about the house had been restored, yet it still had an authentic feel.

"Wait here." The burly man knocked on a door on the right-hand side of the hall and waited a moment before entering. Angus heard muffled voices, one of which was unmistakably Idris.

The door opened and the man nodded to him. "You can go in."

As soon as he walked in, Idris stood up from behind his computer and welcomed him. The room was just like the hall, dominated by exposed beams, and to the left was a large original fireplace.

"Angus, nice to see you again," Idris said, with genuine warmth. He held out his hand and Angus shook it. "Take a seat." He pointed at the chair next to his desk. "Can I get you a drink?"

It had been a long drive, so Angus nodded. "Tea, if you've got it, please."

Idris went to the door and shouted through it. "Cerys, dear, can you bring some tea in here?"

Angus heard the faint "yes" of an old woman's voice. Idris came back and sat behind his desk. "Cerys is my housekeeper. She's getting past it, but she's wonderful. Friend of my aunt. Keeping it in the family, sort of."

Angus nodded and looked at a small bookshelf on the other wall. It contained a few self-help books, a picture frame with the words, "When Nothing Goes Right, Go Left" written inside in calligraphy, and another frame beside it, which read, "If you don't like where you are, then change it. You are not a tree".

Idris leaned back in his chair and looked at Angus. "I'm surprised that you came all this way to speak to me. We could have done it on the phone or Zoom, you know."

"I wanted to talk to you in person."

"Old style, eh? Terrible news about Charlotte. Will she be all right?"

"She will be. She's recovering."

"How did it happen?"

"She was hit by a car in Exeter."

"Nasty." Idris shook his head.

"It was unfortunate."

"Well, fire away, Angus. What did you want to talk to me about?"

Angus took out his notebook and pen. "I wondered if you'd mind going over the kidnapping with me again. I know you've spoken about it already, but I want to go over the details."

"I told you and Mark everything already." Idris waved his hand in a dismissive manner. "Which bit? All of it? Because, to be honest, I'm trying to move on."

Angus nodded. "You said you only ever saw one kidnapper. Are you absolutely sure of that?"

"Yes."

"Did you see any other person after you were taken to the place where you were held?"

"No. I told you all this before." Idris looked aggrieved.

"And you never saw their face?"

"As I told you, no."

Angus took out his phone and showed Idris the still of

Oliver Trent, which Euan had screen-grabbed from TikTok and sent him. "Do you recognise this man?"

Idris examined the image, then shook his head. "Never seen him before."

"Are you sure?"

"Pretty sure. He doesn't look familiar."

"Could he have been an ex-employee at your cybersecurity company?"

"At CI Cyber?" He shook his head again. "I knew all the employees, and he wasn't one of them."

Angus put his phone on the desk. "Does he look anything like the kidnapper?"

"I don't think so. But like I said before, he wore a balaclava the whole time."

"You saw his eyes, though." Angus picked up the phone and held it in front of Idris again. "Look at the eyes."

Idris shook his head yet again, but there was something in the reaction that didn't sit right with Angus, though he couldn't say what.

"You said in the original interview that the kidnapper didn't speak to you except when necessary."

"That's right."

Angus stared at Idris. He was sure he was lying. Then Idris's left eyelid flickered and Angus knew he was hiding something. "Come on, you need to tell me."

"What's the point, Angus? You won't find out who it was if the police can't."

"You'd be surprised." Angus leaned forward. "Tell me what the kidnapper said to you. I want to get to the bottom of why they released you."

Idris glared at him. "So you can accuse me of setting the whole thing up too?"

"I don't think you set the whole thing up. Charlotte

doesn't either. She said you'd never waste police time like that."

Idris leaned back in the chair, looking relieved. He sighed, then rubbed his hand over his face and sat forward. "Look, I did talk to him. I tried to engage with him, to get him to sympathise with me."

Angus opened his mouth, then decided to stay silent and let Idris speak.

"When we got to the garage, he sat me in front of a computer. He had this device, some kind of hard disk, that he wanted me to hack into. Break the encryption. I told him that I didn't know anything about encryption, because I'm not that good with technology."

"What did he do when you told him that?"

"He didn't believe me. He said that I couldn't have found out how to stop the King Imperial virus without some skills. So I told him it was Charlotte who did all that. She was the one who worked out how to stop that one, and loads of others. Bloody genius, she is."

Angus sat bolt upright. "Wait, what?"

"I told him Charlotte was the one with all the tech skills," said Idris. "Well, it's the truth. Credit where credit's due." He smiled. "It might not have worked out with us, but she's always been good at that stuff."

Angus wrote quickly on his notepad as Idris spoke. When he'd got it down, he paused for a moment, thinking of his next question.

"What happened when you explained that to the kidnapper?"

"He started to get angry and said I was a fraud. I thought he was going to kill me. I told him I wasn't a fraud, that I'd worked on the business and admin side while Charlotte did the techie stuff. That we'd worked as a team. That she'd done some kind of decryption on the virus."

"Why did he think it was you who found a fix to the virus?"

Idris looked out of the window. "I don't know."

"You told people you'd found it, didn't you?"

Idris took a deep breath. "Some people assumed it was me, and I didn't deny it."

Angus had tried to judge Idris on his own merits, rather than on what he'd heard or seen on TV. But now he really despised him. "Did he tell you why he wanted the disk decrypted?"

Idris shook his head. "I didn't ask. Didn't want to upset him. He was pretty upset already."

"He still kept you for nearly two days after you told him this."

"He thought I was lying and told me to try to decrypt it. I still thought he was going to kill me. I gave it a go at one point, but I didn't have a clue."

"When he decided to let you go, was that because he'd realised that Charlotte was the techie, and not you?"

That's it. It had been all about getting someone with tech skills. Angus was more certain than ever that the man calling himself Oliver Trent was behind this, and that he was the kidnapper. "Idris, why didn't you tell us this?"

Idris shrugged. "I was embarrassed. How would that look in the papers? I didn't want people to find out that I was released because I don't know much about computers."

Angus shook his head. "Everything's relevant in an investigation."

"Well, it didn't even work, did it, because they thought I staged the whole thing."

"What else did you say about Charlotte?"

"Not much. Just about setting the company up with her, and that we'd divorced."

"What else?"

"Just that we built the business up by helping companies to prevent hacking and other cyberthreats."

Angus finished writing and looked up at Idris, who was studying him. "Is there anything else you haven't told the police that I should know?"

Idris shook his head. "No. Is Charlotte paying you to try and find out who kidnapped me?"

"No."

"Then why are you so keen on finding out every detail?"

Angus pondered whether he should say anything. Then he found he couldn't hold back. "Because I think that whoever kidnapped you is after Charlotte."

Chapter Twenty-One

I dris laughed. "That's stupid. Why would he kidnap her?" His tone was derisive.

Angus glared at him. "Because he thinks she can decrypt the hard drive that you couldn't, maybe?"

"I guess so. You'd better get her to keep an eye out, then."

Angus took a deep breath. It was rare for him to lose his rag, but he was fighting back his anger. Idris must have known the kidnapper would go after Charlotte. It was the logical conclusion.

His thoughts were interrupted by Idris. "So tell me, are you and Charlotte a thing?"

Angus felt himself flush slightly. "We're just work colleagues," he said flatly.

"Right," Idris said in a slightly sarcastic tone.

None of your business anyway, thought Angus.

"Look, I might have cheated on Cha-Cha, but I still care about her. She's the mother of my boys, and for years we had a lot of fun."

Angus stared at him. "You cheated on her."

"It was inevitable. I couldn't resist Michelle: we're like soulmates. It's like she's telepathic. She seems to know my every thought." He lowered his voice and leaned forward. "She sorts me out whenever I want it too. And she's willing to do all sorts of things that Charlotte wouldn't."

Angus squeezed his eyes closed and pushed away the thought of Idris and Charlotte at it. If anything, he was proud that she wouldn't demean herself to Michelle's level. Whatever that was.

Idris stood up and said in a cheery voice, "Is that everything, then?"

Angus nodded and put his notebook and pen into his inside jacket pocket. He needed to get out of there and warn Charlotte.

"Sorry about the tea. Or lack of. Cerys has a habit of forgetting things or falling asleep. She'll probably come in with it as soon as you've gone." He laughed.

Angus stood up and gave him a curt nod, then left.

When he reached his car, he put both hands on the car roof and breathed out. Idris was a prize arsehole, and he had no idea how an intelligent woman like Charlotte could have fallen for him, married him and had children with him. He wanted to punch that smug face. He didn't usually get violent urges, but there were plenty of reasons why he could have just socked Idris one.

He got into his car and dialled Grigore. It rang twice before he picked up.

"I need you to keep a close eye on Charlotte. Don't let anyone we don't know near her, and don't let her out of your sight."

"Okay," said Grigore. "But vhy?"

"I think the kidnapper is after her."

"I vill never leave her side," Grigore assured him.

Next, Angus called Woody and updated him on his conversation with Idris.

"The little shit," said Woody, through gritted teeth. "I knew he was hiding something."

"Can we get police protection for her?"

"You really think he's after her?" said Woody. "I mean, she's not well at the moment. She won't be much use to anyone."

"I don't think he'd care."

"I'll try, but I don't think they'll go for it. Unless there's been a direct threat, it's unlikely."

"Helena is already arranging some private protection."

"Good. Well done, mate. I knew I could rely on you."

"I thought you might think I was paranoid."

"Well, I did wonder if you might have other reasons to protect Charlotte..."

Angus had no answer to that, and he wasn't willing to say anything, so swiftly ended the call.

As he drove back to Exeter, his mind swirled with the possible implications. He was sure Charlotte was in danger; he had to speak to her. He was also sure that Oliver Trent was behind it all, but he needed proof.

Back in Topsham, he was let in by Helena. He asked her and Grigore to come upstairs with him.

"Charlotte, she in bed. She still need sleep," Helena explained.

"Go and see if she's awake. I need to talk to you all."

Helena nodded and went upstairs. After a minute, she came back down. "She awake, and she say you go up."

Angus found Charlotte sitting up in bed, looking pale and tired. Even though he knew she was still recovering from her accident, his heart went out to her.

"What's so urgent, Angus?" She was propped up by a

130

multitude of pillows.

"I've just been to visit Idris." He explained their discussion.

"Yes, he was never into the technical detail," said Charlotte. "He left all that to me."

"But since he's been on *Vipers' Nest*, Idris has given the impression that he's a tech genius," Angus replied.

"Well, you would know. You've been watching it." She thought for a moment. "Do you think the kidnapper is just a crazed fan who needs help with something?"

"Idris said he never mentioned the show. But that doesn't mean he isn't a fan."

"It does seem suspicious, Angus. This whole kidnapping thing has been so strange, from start to finish." She closed her eyes.

Angus took her hand for a moment, which made her open them. "I don't think it has finished, Charlotte. I think the kidnapper is going after you next. Idris told them you were the one who did the tech stuff. Why else would he suddenly release Idris when he discovered that he had no tech skills at all? And another thing. Idris said the kidnapper didn't believe him at first, because he knew your company had found their way around lots of encrypted viruses."

Charlotte stared at him, processing what he'd just said.

Angus addressed the room. "Can you think of anyone else who might hold a grudge against Charlotte? It could be anything. It could be something to do with the company before it was sold."

Grigore remained quiet, but Helena came forward and sat on the end of the bed. "Remember zat terrible virus attack on city stock exchange, and you found solution. Not zat you got much for it. Vut it called?"

Angus consulted his notebook. "The King Imperial virus?"

"Yez! Zat's it."

"That was years ago, though," said Charlotte, with a frown.

"Tell me about it."

Charlotte picked up the glass on her bedside table and took a sip of water. "It was a virus that infected the London Stock Exchange: a nasty one. It spread really quickly and encrypted all the data."

Angus frowned. "Like ransomware?"

"Angus, have you been learning cybersecurity?" Charlotte's mouth curved in a sly smile.

"No, but I'm not such a technophobe that I don't know the basics of viruses."

"It wasn't quite ransomware. They encrypted the data but didn't ask for money. They just wanted to cause havoc. Normal ransomware wants money, and they'll decrypt your data if you pay them. Anyway, I worked on the virus with a small team and figured out the decryption key. That meant game over: the virus was useless from then on. I put the decryption key on the internet, too, so that anyone who got the virus in future would be able to fix it."

"Do you know who was behind it?"

"No idea. You hardly ever do. Some people who create viruses have a tag, but this one didn't."

"How would the kidnapper know about the King Imperial virus? Was it mentioned in the press?"

"The stock market going down was in the papers, but I'm not sure what the name of the virus was."

"I'll get Euan to check." Angus took out his phone and texted him.

"You'll be happy to know I've spoken to Ross and he's

arranged an armed guard for me," said Charlotte. "They should be here in forty-eight hours."

Angus sighed and Charlotte looked at him. "What?"

"Is that the soonest they can get here?"

"Yes."

"I was hoping they'd come immediately. Forgive me, but I'd have thought that with all your money, you could get people to do what you want as soon as you want it."

"Do you really think I need protection? I'm sure this was just someone who wanted help."

"I want you to go into hiding until the armed guard arrives," Angus told her.

"Really?" She folded her arms. "Are you sure you're not being paranoid? My home is safer than being out there."

"I'm being cautious. Nothing wrong with cautious."

"You're basing all this on a hunch."

"Possibly. But my hunches are usually right."

She narrowed her eyes. "I don't think it's a good idea. Where would I go?"

"Out of the country would be my preference. Can't you hire a private jet to take you somewhere exotic?"

"I could... Costa Rica is lovely at this time of year."

"You could go to refuge," Helena suggested.

"The one on Dartmoor?" Angus asked. "No. It needs to be somewhere unconnected to you. Pick a holiday cottage or a hotel. But don't book it in your real name, obviously."

"You want me to go full stealth?" There was a smile on her lips.

"What?" Angus pushed his glasses up his nose.

"You've never been protective like this before. Is this your primal male coming out?"

Angus shrugged. "You're my friend and work partner. I need your techie skills, among other things. Now is the time to tell me that you have a panic room installed somewhere in this house."

"Sorry to disappoint you, but no. I'm not completely paranoid."

"Too bad."

He turned to Helena. "Take Charlotte somewhere, get a burner phone, and come back when the armed guard arrives."

Charlotte grinned. "Wow, you really are going full stealth. Burner phone?"

"It's what you use to do all your hacking," he said, in a dry tone. "But get a new one, just in case."

"I have lots of burner phones I haven't used yet."

"Let me know the number, but otherwise, don't tell anyone."

"I vill pack for you," said Helena. "Vhere we go?"

"We'll drive for a while, then pick a hotel that looks half-decent. Preferably one with a spa. Not that I'll be able to use it with this." She pointed to her cast. "I'm just about able to move around, but crutches are much harder to use than you'd think."

"Pay in cash," Angus said.

Charlotte raised her eyebrows. "Does anyone even take cash any more?"

"Plenty do." Angus moved to the door. "If I'm wrong, you can berate me for evermore. I hope I am." He left the room without waiting for her answer. He was sure he wasn't being paranoid, but this was a nightmare. Charlotte thought he was mad and she was just humouring him. Why, she wasn't sure. Maybe because she was unwell.

But the worst of it was that he had no idea how to find Oliver Trent. If the police, with all their resources, couldn't do it, how could he?

Chapter Twenty-Two

The pain in Charlotte's leg woke her the next morning. The small amount of light getting past the curtains allowed her to look around the unfamiliar room. A wave of panic went through her. For a moment she wondered if she had been kidnapped, then she remembered Angus's plan for her to hide.

She was in a grotty bedroom somewhere near Crediton, just north of Exeter. It was a budget motel, privately owned, and there were vacancies for a reason. Only the truly desperate would want to stay here. The room was tiny, and looked like it had last been decorated decades ago. The bathroom had a toilet, sink and shower, and although it was clean, they needed ripping out and replacing with something made this century.

The night before, Helena had packed them both suitcases and driven until they found it. "Too obvious to pick expensive hotel," Helena said, as she pulled up outside.

"I don't think this is a good idea," Charlotte replied. "I hate poky little hotels. This one looks dodgy too."

Helena had dismissed her protestations. "You put up vith it. Better zan hospital."

"Do you think Angus is being paranoid?"

Helena shrugged. "Maybe, but better safe zan sorry."

A few hours later, Charlotte had fallen asleep watching TV.

The following morning, not only did her leg ache, but it was a struggle to get up and use the bathroom. The cast made it difficult to do everything. She wondered how she'd cope with weeks and weeks before it came off.

Had Angus gone completely mad? Here she was, hiding in a hotel room, with armed guards on the way. She wondered whether Oliver Trent could be the kidnapper, and whether he was behind it all. She knew she hadn't met him before, but it would explain the strange way he'd looked at her that day, and his keenness to get them both to drink coffee.

She looked over at Helena in the other bed, fast asleep and snoring gently. The only other sound was Charlotte's stomach rumbling.

She switched on the TV and flicked through a few channels. One was broadcasting an episode of *Vipers' Nest*. "Great." Charlotte rolled her eyes, but she didn't change the channel.

Unfortunately, it was an episode with Idris. The Vipers were being pitched a small-business idea by a young woman in her twenties. She wore a smock pinafore dress with two large pockets on the front and stood next to some mannequins wearing similar dresses of different colours.

"Good afternoon, Vipers. My name is Amanda, and I run a small business called We Want Pockets. I make clothes for women, all of which have large pockets. All the materials used are ethically sourced and I only use natural fibres. I'm after a hundred thousand pounds for ten percent of the business."

Charlotte watched, interested.

First up to quiz her was the only female Viper, Sally Hicks."How long have you been trading?"

"Three years," Amanda replied.

"How many have you sold in your last financial year?"

Amanda lifted her chin in pride. "Nearly three thousand."

Sally nodded. "And what is the markup for each item?"

In turn, the Vipers questioned Amanda about her business. Idris was last, sitting with an empty notebook and pen. He put the end of the pen to his mouth, then said, "I've listened with interest, Amanda, but I have to say, I'm not keen on the style. Are you planning any other lines of clothes?"

Amanda smiled. "Yes. I plan to have shorts, trousers, smock tops, bikinis and swimsuits. Even wedding dresses." She laughed.

"Wedding dresses with pockets?" Idris stared at her. Charlotte knew that look. It was distaste. "Look, your clothing is nice enough but I just can't see a mass market for it. Women like to emphasise their curves and show them off, don't they." It was a statement, not a question. "Why would you want to hide them behind massive godforsaken pockets? Anyway, women have handbags. They don't need pockets."

Amanda's face fell.

"Sorry, petal, but I'm out. I don't want to be 'out of pocket' by investing in you." He shook his head.

The presenter provided a voice-over as Amanda walked out. "Not the reception Amanda was hoping for. With Idris Beavin out, that's it for Amanda and her pockets."

The shot changed to Amanda outside the Viper building, being interviewed by the presenter. "Are you disappointed?"

Amanda was clearly holding back tears, but smiled. "Of course I am, but I'll keep going. I believe in my product, and the feedback I've had from my customers means I won't stop."

The programme cut to a commercial break. Charlotte picked up her burner phone and went to the We Love Pockets website. She made a mental note to order something when she got home.

Angus knocked on Euan's bedroom door and went in. "Euan, I need you to do something for me."

He was in the middle of a shooting game on the laptop, too absorbed to notice Angus. Rubbish littered the floor, and the room stank of stale teenager. He was wearing large headphones with a microphone attached. "Shoot him!" he said into the mic. "Round the back of the hut, come on..."

The screen showed his army avatar running around in what looked like a war zone. Angus moved closer. "Euan, I need you to do something for me."

Euan glanced at Angus, then turned back to the game and fired his gun at the soldier in front of him. There was an explosion and the game ended.

"I'm dead," he said to whoever he was playing with. He took off his headphones and looked at Angus properly. "All right, Uncle Ang."

"I said that I need you to do something for me."

"Yeah, I know. Clean the bathroom. I was just about to do it."

"The bathroom can wait. I need you to do something on that." He indicated the laptop.

"Cool."

"I need you to find the owner of the Airbnb that Oliver Trent used."

"Okay."

Euan began typing and the Airbnb website appeared. He searched for the property Oliver Trent had used. "Is this it?"

"That's the one," said Angus.

Euan clicked on the listing. "It says here that the property is hosted by Jennifer Parker."

"Wait, what?" Angus turned the screen towards him to look at the host photo. "That's the nurse from the other day. The one who was looking after Charlotte."

Euan clicked on the small round photo. "Her profile says, 'Hi, I'm Jen. I'm a part-time nurse, and love hosting travellers'."

Angus pushed his glasses up his nose. "That's no coincidence."

He went downstairs, his mind in a whirl. Could Jen be connected to Oliver Trent? He needed to talk to Fiona: she had arranged the nurses. He rang her number but there was no answer. *She must be at work.* He rang the main number at the hospital and asked to be put through to Fiona, but was told that she was in theatre and wouldn't be out for hours.

He went back upstairs to Euan. "I need you to find out as much as you can about Jennifer Parker."

"Just like I did with Oliver Trent?"

"Yes, but I think Jennifer Parker is a real person."

Euan began typing rapidly. Angus watched him, frowning. "Did Charlotte teach you how to hack?" he asked.

Euan didn't look up. "Of course not, Uncle Angus. Hacking's illegal." But the smile on Euan's lips told him otherwise. Angus considered asking Euan to hack into

Jennifer's Airbnb account, but dismissed the idea. Getting a minor to illegally hack a website was a step too far: Duncan would never speak to him again. He needed Charlotte for that, but he wasn't going to contact her unless it was absolutely necessary.

An hour later, Angus was on his way to Jennifer's address: a house in the village of Christow, on the edge of Dartmoor and close to the Airbnb. Christow was one of the most sought-after locations in Devon. Euan had found her address quickly, and more importantly, without breaking the law. Jennifer's house was a mid-terrace in the centre of the village. He parked farther up the road and knocked on the door.

A moment later, Jen opened it. It took her a moment to recognise him. When she did, she tried to close the door, but Angus put his foot in the way. He pushed his way in and she retreated into the hall. "What do you want?" She was dressed in black sweatpants and an oversized pale-green T-shirt.

Angus closed the front door behind him. "I want to know how you know Oliver Trent – or whoever he really is."

"Never heard of him." Her voice and face were deadpan.

"Really? You're going to try that one, are you?"

Jen bolted into the lounge and Angus followed. She grabbed her mobile phone. "Get out, or I'll call the police."

Angus shrugged. "Call them if you like. I'm sure they'll be interested to hear about your connection with the man who abducted Idris Beavin."

"Look, I didn't know he was behind that. Not at first." She took a step back.

"Just tell me where he is."

"I don't know."

Angus indicated the chair beside her. "Sit down. I just want information about Oliver Trent. Then I'll go."

She eyed him warily, then did as he asked. Angus sat down opposite her. "What's his real name?"

Jen breathed deeply: she was deciding whether or not to tell him. "Nathan Fisher," she said eventually.

"And how do you know him?"

"He's my daughter's father. We're not together. Not any more."

"Why did he use your Airbnb house?"

"He was staying there for a few days. He does sometimes when he's visiting Isla."

"Isla is your daughter?"

"Yeah."

Angus looked around and saw a few toys in the corner of the room. "How did you come to own two Airbnbs when you work part-time as a nurse?"

"You mean how can I afford it? I inherited one of them and money from my aunt. She didn't have any children. I decided to rent the house out and bought the other with her savings." There was resentment in her voice at having to explain.

Angus nodded. "When did you know that he'd kidnapped Idris Beavin?"

Jen's eyes darted around the room. Angus grew impatient. "Come on, tell me. Think of your nursing career."

She looked him in the eye. "Not until after he'd let him go. He came here in the middle of the night, panicking. He said he needed someone good with tech, because people were after him for money he owed."

It's always about money, thought Angus. "Did he tell you anything else?"

"He said that he'd taken Idris and tried to get him to decrypt something, but he couldn't. He called him a useless cretin." Angus felt that was an accurate description of Idris. "He said that if he didn't get it decrypted he was a dead man."

Angus took out his notebook and wrote down Nathan's name. "Are you sure he didn't say what was encrypted?"

She shook her head.

"Did he ask you to help him?"

"Not with the decryption: I wouldn't have a clue about that sort of stuff." She snorted. "He just asked to use the Airbnb so that he could get someone there to help him."

"Did he tell you how he planned to do that, or who it was?"

"No. I just thought he was going to hire someone. Then the next day, he told me to make sure I got the nursing job to look after Charlotte in Topsham. That was easy, because the nursing agency owed me a few favours."

"You didn't ask him why he wanted you to work there? Or how he knew about it?" Angus felt himself growing angry at how easily it had all been set up.

She closed her eyes for a moment. "I didn't ask how he knew. Sometimes, with Nathan, it's better not to know how he finds things out. He told me she was a cybersecurity expert, and he needed her help."

"What did he tell you to do when you were nursing Charlotte?"

"Not much. Just keep an eye on her, and tell him when she was alone, so that he could come in and get her to decrypt it. But she was never alone: there were people around all the time. I was glad. I didn't like spying on her. When Nathan said he needed Charlotte to decrypt some-thing, I told him to just ask her. But he said he couldn't trust her to do it out of goodwill, because it was too valuable."

"Why did you help him?"

"He was desperate. I don't love him any more, but I want my daughter to know her father while she's growing up. I never knew mine."

Angus studied her face, which was full of remorse. She clearly hadn't realised what she'd been getting into or that it was too late to back out. "Do you know where he is now? He isn't here, is he?"

"No. He stayed the night, but when I woke up this morning, he'd gone."

"Did he say what he was going to do?"

"No."

Angus assessed whether Jen was telling the truth. Nathan could be upstairs right now. But if Jen was lying, she was a very good actress.

He stood up. "If he contacts you, call me straight away."

She nodded.

Outside, he paused by his car. He needed to find Nathan, and there wasn't much he could do on his own.

First, though, he needed to talk to Charlotte. The call went to voicemail, so he left a message. "It's me. Oliver Trent is actually called Nathan Fisher. He's on the loose and he's after you. You need to hold tight and make sure you stay hidden more than ever. Call me back when you get this."

Next, he phoned Woody, to update him on Oliver Trent's real name and his connection to Jen.

"Good work, Angus. Stay on the line and I'll do a database check on him." Angus heard Woody typing in the background. A few moments later, Woody spoke. "Well, well, well. He has a record with quite a few things on it, but nothing major. ABH a few years ago, some domestic disturbances five years ago, but no prosecutions. The complainant was Jennifer Parker."

"She said that they're not together any more," said Angus. "I wonder if she's being coerced into helping him?"

"There haven't been any further complaints," said Woody. "But that doesn't mean that he isn't influencing her in some way."

"They have a daughter together, so it's possible he's been using that to make her get involved."

"I'll get some female officers round to see what she says. She'll have to come in anyway, if she knew he kidnapped Idris and didn't say anything. I'll get hold of Fiona, too, though she'll have no idea about any of this. There's no way she'd have hired anyone who might put Charlie in danger."

Chapter Twenty-Three

Charlotte flicked from channel to channel on the motel room TV. There was another episode of *Vipers' Nest*, but she couldn't face watching it. She was seriously bored. She'd never gone this long without using a computer, and chastised herself for not checking that Helena had packed her laptop.

She was also hungry, and that wasn't helping. Hangry, more like. Helena was out getting supplies, and she would eat whatever she brought back. She'd asked for pizza, but Helena had insisted on something healthier, especially as Charlotte couldn't exercise until the cast came off. Charlotte knew she should be glad that Helena was looking out for her, but all the same, a bit of pizza wouldn't do any harm.

Her burner phone beeped and she picked it up. It was Angus's number.

You need to leave now. He knows where you are. No time to explain. Meet me at Ide Church car park ASAP.

Charlotte sat bolt upright, her heart pounding. She

typed a reply: *Helena is out getting food; I'll have to wait for her.*

It was half a minute before he replied. *All right, but get out as quickly as you can.*

Charlotte phoned Helena but she didn't answer. *She must be driving.* She opened her maps app and looked for the car park. Ide was a small village just outside West Exeter, and although she didn't know it very well, she'd been through it a few times.

She grabbed her crutches, stood up and started packing. It was tricky, and she ended up dumping most of the clothes into the case.

It was another twenty minutes before Helena came in. She was carrying a takeaway bag from a noodle restaurant. It smelt divine.

"Vat you doing?" she said, the moment she saw that Charlotte was out of bed. "You should rest."

Charlotte told her about the text from Angus.

"He no text me."

"Does he normally text you?"

"No, but he zaid he vould."

"Maybe he forgot."

"How far Ide?"

"Not far. It'll take about twenty minutes to get there."

"I finish pack, you eat."

Charlotte didn't argue; she was starving. She sat on the edge of the bed and devoured a large spring roll. The noodles would have to wait.

When Helena had finished, she gave the room a quick once-over and they left. At the car park, Charlotte looked around for anyone suspicious. Oliver Trent could be in any car. A few cars were parked, but they were all empty. They got into Helena's car and set off.

There wasn't much traffic, so it took them twenty minutes to get to Ide. The medieval church was made of stone and larger than Charlotte remembered. But when they pulled into the church car park, it was empty.

Helena stopped the car. "I have bad feeling. Angus no here."

"He'll come any minute, I'm sure." Charlotte sent him a text: *We're here.*

A few moments later, a transit van sped into the car park and parked diagonally in front of them, blocking their exit.

The driver was wearing a balaclava. He got out and tried to open the passenger door, but it was locked.

"Unlock the door or I'll shoot you through the window!" He pointed a handgun at Charlotte.

She did as he asked.

"Get out!" he yelled.

Helena screamed, and Charlotte put her hands up.

"Get out!" he yelled again.

"I-I need the crutches. They're in the back."

The man looked at her plaster cast, then the crutches. Keeping the gun trained on her, he opened the back door, picked up the crutches and gave them to Charlotte. He took a step back. All the time Helena was whimpering. "Get in the van," he commanded.

Charlotte looked at his eyes, the only part of him which showed through the tiny slit of the balaclava, and recognised Oliver Trent. She lifted her leg out of the car and hoisted herself up.

"No!" shouted Helena.

"I'll be all right," Charlotte replied. "He just wants me to decrypt something. Don't you, Oliver? If that's your real name." She spoke to reassure herself, as well as Helena, and

147

felt her heart rate increase, a secret acknowledgement that she was in danger. Angus's concerned face flashed in front of her. She should have taken his worries over her safety more seriously. She wondered how Oliver knew.

"Why don't you take me home, bring whatever you want decrypting, and I'll do it for you."

"Shut up!" he shouted.

Charlotte bent down and spoke to Helena. "Try not to worry."

"She's coming with us," he shouted.

Charlotte narrowed her eyes. "No, she isn't. If you want me to decrypt whatever it is you want decrypted, she stays where she is." She leaned against the car and folded her arms.

The gun in his hand wavered as he considered this. "Get in the van," he said, a moment later.

Charlotte hobbled to the van and got in.

Oliver aimed the gun at Helena, then as Charlotte closed the door, he shot at one of Helena's tyres, puncturing it.

She heard Helena scream.

Then he got in the van and they drove off.

Chapter Twenty-Four

"Where are you taking me?" Charlotte asked as they headed out of Ide.

"Shut up."

"That isn't very nice. If you want me to hack something for you, you could at least be polite."

He glanced at her, but said nothing.

"You could at least tell me your real name. I know it isn't Oliver Trent."

"It's none of your business."

That was encouraging. If he was planning to kill her, he'd have no qualms about admitting his real identity.

She decided to stay quiet for the time being, and it wasn't long before he was heading on to Dartmoor. "Have you got another Airbnb?" she asked.

He didn't reply, but ten minutes later they pulled up outside a small cottage in the middle of nowhere, with a slate roof and white rendered walls.

Inside, it was one big room on the ground floor. The kitchen was at the rear, and the front looked like a show home. It was definitely an Airbnb.

"Over there," he barked.

She hobbled to the small dining table and sat down. He went to the cupboard and pulled out a laptop, then put a removable hard disk on the table. "Break the encryption on this and I won't kill you: I'll let you go. If you can't do it, you'll have to pay me a hundred million." He took off the balaclava, and even though she knew his face, it was still a shock to see it.

"What's on it?"

"Stop asking questions. It's none of your business."

Charlotte folded her arms. "Then I won't help you. I'm not getting involved with anything dodgy."

"It isn't dodgy."

"Then why have you kidnapped me? You could just have asked me to help you."

"Because then..." He wagged his finger at her. "Oh no, you're not going to find out."

"Then you won't get into the hard disk." She pursed her lips, thinking. "Anyway, I can't help you. You need an encryption expert. I'm not one of those."

"You're a hacker, aren't you?"

"Yes, but not a cryptologist. I mean, I know some cryptology, but not much."

He stared at her. "You're lying."

"I'm not."

"Yes, you are. You hacked my ransomware. *You*. You broke through it."

"Wait, what?"

He started pacing the room. Charlotte watched his agitated movement. "I know you can break the decryption, because you broke my King Imperial virus." He pointed to the hard drive. "If I don't decrypt it, they'll kill me. And probably my daughter too."

"Who's 'they'?"

"Bad people."

"That goes without saying. What did you do to them?"

"Nothing. They want me to decrypt that." He pointed at the disk again.

Charlotte picked up the hard disk and turned it in her hands, examining it. It was a solid-state disk with no moving parts. All the data was held on chips. Unlike a magnetic hard disk, the data would eventually be lost, but that would take years.

"Is it cryptocurrency passwords?"

He stopped pacing, then gave a small nod.

She wondered why anyone would leave their cryptocurrency password on a hard disk. She'd have chosen a magnetic disk. "I take it you've tried to decrypt it?"

"Of course I have."

"And you thought Idris could do it?"

"I did, but he's a useless bastard."

"Well, not totally useless. He was fantastic at changing nappies when the boys were babies. And he's really good at swimming." She opened the laptop. "Log me in, and I'll see what I can do."

Oliver walked over and typed the password into the laptop, and the desktop appeared.

Charlotte plugged the disk into the laptop. "If I'm going to try and decrypt it, I need access to the internet."

"Not happening. You'll alert someone."

Charlotte considered. "Well, if you watch, you'll stop me from doing that, won't you? I need access to GitHub: all my code is stored on there."

"Someone will see that you've logged into it, and they'll trace the IP address to here."

"Not if I use a VPN." Charlotte looked up at him. "You

really don't trust me, do you? But you'll have to let me access it, or I can't help."

He studied her, then nodded. "Do it, but don't forget I'm watching you. I'll hurt you if you try anything." He tethered his mobile phone to the computer.

Charlotte was starting to get the impression that his threats were empty ones. Then again, she was in the middle of nowhere with a plaster cast on one leg. She was his last hope, but given his desperation, it was best to keep quiet and get on with the job. Her mind raced. How could she alert someone to where she was?

"I'll have to amend my low-level code to run the encryption algorithms over it," she said. "Did you try any yourself?"

"I've never done low level, but I tried a few: AES, DES, RSA, Blowfish, Twofish."

Charlotte nodded. "Well, I hope you won't mind if I try them too. Most hard disks use AES. Who owns the disk?"

"I told you, that's no concern of yours."

"It is, because if I know more about them, it might help me decrypt it."

"It won't."

"All right, I admit that I'm trying to phish, but you should at least tell me some of it. Did you steal it?" She watched his reaction. "You didn't steal it."

"No."

She started typing again. "So it was you behind the King Imperial virus." *Helena was right.*

"Yeah."

"Wow. Did you target the stock market on purpose?"

"Yeah, I lost a load of money on there. They deserved it."

As they chatted, Charlotte clicked on the computer to

find her decryption code. "But I came along and stopped it. Does that mean you hate me?"

He shrugged.

"You made one stupid mistake, of course," said Charlotte. "You wrote your own encryption. That's just stupid. Everyone in cryptography knows that writing your own encryption is like tweeting your bank password to the world. Established encryption algorithms are tested and retested. What you needed was one of those ones with a long key."

"You're an insufferable know-it-all, aren't you? Stop talking and get coding."

"It's programming."

"What?"

"It's called programming. Coding is a common term these days, but it sounds ridiculously amateurish."

"Fine. Stop talking and get programming."

"Thank you. I will." Charlotte turned back to her code.

Chapter Twenty-Five

Angus arrived home to find Euan back on his computer game. He didn't have the energy to get him off it, so left him to it. He wasn't sure what to do while he waited for the police to find Nathan. He wanted to get out there and help, but there wasn't much he could do.

A few hours later, his phone rang. He picked it up, expecting Charlotte. Even though she wasn't supposed to contact him, he suspected she wouldn't be able to keep that promise. But to his surprise, the display showed it was Helena.

"Charlotte gone, he got her!" she cried as soon as he answered.

"What!"

"He send text. He pretend he you, he make us meet in church car park Ide and he take her. He shoot my car wheel so I no follow." She burst into tears.

Angus stood rooted to the spot. "How did he pretend he was me?"

"He text, it your number. I still at car park in Ide."

"Have you called the police?"

"No, I call you first."

"All right, I'll call Woody. You call Grigore. I'll come and get you. Was he in the same van as when he kidnapped Idris?"

"I zink so."

Angus's brain was in a spin. All he could think about was that Charlotte was in danger and his worst fears had come true.

When he got to the church car park at Ide, Grigore was there already. Moments later, Woody pulled up in an unmarked car.

Angus went straight to Helena who was hugging Grigore. "I vill kill him," Grigore said over Helena's head.

"Not if I get to him first," Angus replied.

Woody nodded to Angus. "Which way did he drive, Helena?"

Helena explained, and Woody took out his phone, dialled a number and started barking commands.

"He kill her, I know he vill," Helena said between sobs, then she let go of Grigore.

"He needs her to decrypt something," said Angus. "He won't kill her." But Angus's head was filled with the same doubts. *What if...*

"She good at decryption." Helena sniffed. "He kill her after."

"We'll find her before that," said Angus. "In the meantime, we need to get your car back on the road. Have you got a spare?"

"Yez."

Angus and Grigore headed to the boot and Woody examined the bullet hole in the tyre. "I'll need that as evidence."

After they'd changed the wheel, Helena assured them that she could drive to Charlotte's house. She and Grigore were determined to wait there for news.

When Angus got home, he debated whether or not he should tell Euan. On the one hand, Euan should be told the truth. On the other, he wanted to protect him. In the end, it was Euan who started the conversation when he'd asked what was happening with the case. Angus had told him everything, and Euan's reaction had been the same as his – anguish and anxiety.

Angus wondered whether he would go insane with worry. His heart was racing, he couldn't eat and he was struggling even to drink water. All he could think about was Charlotte and whether she was still alive. What was Nathan doing to her? He wanted her to decrypt the disk, and Angus was sure that she'd be able to do it. But what then?

Or what if she couldn't decrypt it? What would Nathan do to her? Would he let her go, as he had Idris? Or would he get angry and hurt her? However much Angus tried to stop thoughts like that crowding in, he couldn't.

He sat down, then stood up and paced, waiting for his phone to ring, but it stayed silent. Occasionally he would get a text from Helena, asking for news, but nothing else. He flicked through the TV channels to distract himself, but it didn't work.

"Uncle Angus?" Euan was standing in the doorway.

"Hi Euan, you okay? How's the battle going?" Angus asked, referring to the game he'd been playing.

"Yeah, good. Look—"

"Have you eaten?"

"Yeah. Uncle Angus, something weird's going on."

Euan shifted from foot to foot. "It might be nothing, but I keep getting this text message on my phone..."

Angus frowned. "What phone? Your dad took yours away."

Euan shrugged. "Charlotte lent me a phone. I need it for the course she's got me doing. She said it's a burner phone she uses sometimes." He pulled it out of his pocket.

Angus rubbed his jaw. *One day, when all this is over, and Charlotte's safe, I'll have words with her about this.* "So what's the message?" he asked.

"'Famous.tools.crass.' It keeps arriving every minute from a blocked number." Euan gave Angus the phone and he saw a string of texts, each saying the same thing.

"When did they start?"

"About twenty minutes ago."

"And there are no other messages?"

"No."

"Could it be some sort of reminder? Something Charlotte set up on the phone? Or is it spam?"

"It doesn't look like either of those." Euan's brow furrowed, and suddenly he stared at Angus. "I think I know what it is. What3Words."

Angus stared back. "What three words? What is it, a guessing game?"

That made Euan grin. "No! You know, that app that lets you find a location anywhere in the world without coordinates. You put three words in and it pinpoints the location within ten metres. All the emergency services use it."

Angus hadn't heard of the app; it must have been brought in after he left the police. He made a mental note to install the app: it sounded useful. "Can you look up the location?"

Euan nodded and his thumbs flew over the screen of his phone. "It's on Dartmoor, not far from Ide."

He held out the phone to Angus. "The location shows a house. Do you think it's Charlotte telling us where she is? It's not a coincidence, is it?"

Hope surged through Angus. "Euan, you beauty! Of course it's her. I'll phone Woody, and we'll get going."

Chapter Twenty-Six

They met in a lay-by half a mile from the location the app had indicated. Woody was in an unmarked police car, but a van was there, too, with an armed response unit. They planned to approach the building by foot, to avoid alerting Nathan.

"One of my boys did a check, and it's an Airbnb," said Woody. "Looks like he's rented it for a few days."

Angus nodded. "Not exactly what the owners had in mind, I'll bet."

"Never mind them. He'll wish he'd never been born when I get my hands on him." Woody's voice was grim, and Angus knew he meant every word.

Angus followed the team as they made their way down the lane, moving in on the house. Nathan's van was parked on the drive.

The lead officer of the unit motioned to some of his team to move around the back of the building. A couple of minutes later, he shouted, "Armed police, open up." Then he gave his remaining officers the nod and they attacked the door with a battering ram. After two hits, the door gave way and the officers swarmed in, Woody and Angus heading straight after them.

By the time they got into the room, Nathan was kneeling on the floor with his hands on his head. Charlotte stood by the table, looking down on him.

"Did he hurt you?" Angus asked, concern written all over his face.

"Angus!" She threw herself at him in a hug and he caught her just before she fell over. "I'm fine. Although I could do with some painkillers. My leg is throbbing." Angus reluctantly let her go and she beamed at him. "Euan got my messages, then?"

He nodded. "I have no idea how you did it, but yes, he did."

"Smart lad, that Euan. I wrote a low-level program to automatically text him. Oliver told me early on that he couldn't write in a programming language like that, so he couldn't tell what I was doing. He watched me the whole time as I encoded the message and sent it, but he had no idea." Charlotte reluctantly pulled away from Angus and looked smugly at Nathan, now lying facedown on the floor.

"I hate to interrupt you two, but it's my turn now." Woody stepped forward. "If he's hurt you, I'll make him wish he'd never been born," Woody said into her ear as he bear-hugged her.

"He didn't. I promise."

Woody let her go, too, and they turned to watch as Nathan was handcuffed and hoisted to his feet.

"Is there anyone else, or was it just him?" Woody asked.

"Just him," said Charlotte. "He needed me to decrypt a hard drive with cryptocurrency on it. I haven't managed it yet, but give me a bit more time, and maybe some coffee and food, and I will. Oh, and those painkillers." She indicated the laptop and disk. "He didn't harm me. He couldn't: he needed me too much. Although he wasn't very nice to me." She said the last bit to Nathan's face with a distinct smirk.

"They'll kill me," Nathan said to the room. "They'll get me in prison. They know people."

Charlotte looked at Woody and raised her eyebrows.

Woody nodded, then turned to Nathan. "Well, if you're a good boy and tell us everything you know about who *they* are, we can protect you. Let's get you down to the station."

The officer standing next to Nathan nudged him and led him away. Charlotte sat down on the nearest chair and let out a big sigh.

The following evening, Charlotte, Angus, Euan, Woody, Fiona, Helena and Grigore all sat at Charlotte's dinner table, enjoying a Chinese takeaway. Helena had wanted to cook for them all, but Charlotte had insisted she rest after the trauma of the day before. There had been protestations, but in the end, what Charlotte wanted, Charlotte got.

When they'd finished most of the food, Woody turned the conversation to Nathan. "He admitted everything at the station, eventually. He was too scared of the gang who were after him to say anything at first. But the cyber department sent the disk to GCHQ and they decrypted it. They explained what the encryption was, but it was all gobbledy-gook to me."

Charlotte put her fork down. "Email me the report. I'd love to know which encryption they used."

"I will. Anyway, it didn't contain a hundred million pounds in cryptocurrency."

"Really? Oliver...I mean, Nathan said they were forcing him to decrypt it to write off a debt he owed them."

161

"Let me finish, Charlie. It didn't contain a hundred million pounds in cryptocurrency. It was a hundred *billion*."

Everyone looked at each other in shock.

"Wow," said Charlotte. "That is a *lot* of money. That gang won't be happy when they find out."

"Nope. He'll have to strike a deal and go into witness protection. His daughter too."

"What will happen to the money?"

"The money will go to the Treasury if they find out that the rightful owners are gang members. Let's hope our elected representatives don't waste it." Woody took a sip of his beer. "And he did force Jen into helping. She came in and gave a statement admitting her part in it, but she's going to claim coercive control."

"How he make text look like from Angus?" Helena asked.

Woody sat back and rubbed his stomach. "He cloned Angus's phone when he visited Jen. Apparently he was hiding upstairs."

"Damn it!" cried Angus. "I nearly went up to look for him, but Jen swore he wasn't there. She's a good liar." He looked at Charlotte. "If I'd checked, you wouldn't have been kidnapped." He lowered his voice. "I'm so sorry."

"She claims she didn't know what Nathan was planning," said Woody.

"And you believe her?" Angus shot back.

"I'm not sure. She did tell you his real name and what he was after, so I'm inclined to believe her."

Charlotte shifted in her seat. "This cast is starting to get on my nerves. I'm not sure I can manage week after week of it."

Charlotte's comment reminded Angus of something.

"Did he admit to pushing Charlotte into the path of the car?"

"He claims it was an accident and he lost his footing."

Charlotte snorted.

"He had been following her, though," Woody continued. "He put a tracking device in her coat pocket when they met. His plan was to kidnap her then. He'd put MDMA in Angus's coffee and he was going to do the same to Charlie's, but she didn't have a drink. Luckily Grigore was outside too."

Charlotte closed her eyes and exhaled. "My goodness. Remind me never to accept a coffee from anyone again. I'm making my own from now on. He really needed my help, didn't he?" She poured herself more water.

"Would you have helped him if he'd just asked you?" Euan asked.

Charlotte shook her head. "No. I'd never help anyone with gangland stuff. They make their money from drugs and prostitution, and that's probably the nicer side of it. I'd never enable that." She smiled at him. "I'm very grateful to you, Euan. You worked it out quickly; I knew you would. You've got a glittering career ahead of you if you want it."

Euan beamed.

"If you're interested in a cybersecurity apprenticeship, I could sort one out for you. You'd get paid and learn at the same time."

"Really?" Euan's grin widened. "That would be ace." His face fell. "I failed my exam, though."

"Ingenuity, persistence and problem solving matter, not just exams. Anyway, you can retake the exams while you're working. The pay's excellent too: cybersecurity is one of the best-paid areas in computing. Talk to your mum and dad, then let me know, but the offer's there. You did well working out that message and I'll always be grateful."

Euan blushed.

They sat in silence until Woody spoke. "While I think of it, have you heard from your ex?"

Charlotte sat up straight. "No. But that's fine with me."

Helena stood up and went to her bag. "He sell story to *Hiya Hun* magazine." She rummaged, then held up a glossy celebrity magazine. On the cover was Idris sitting on a high-backed chair, his legs crossed, looking like a king on a throne. Michelle was dressed in a white power suit, her hair and makeup flawless.

"Oh dear." Charlotte grimaced. "Go on, let me read it."

Helena passed it over and Charlotte read out the article:

"*Hiya Hun* magazine exclusive: Idris Beavin has new lease of life after kidnap nightmare.

"Exclusive photos and interview with Idris Beavin and his glamorous wife, Michelle, in their London penthouse.

"After a tumultuous few weeks, Idris Beavin relaxes in his exclusive London suite, located on one of the top floors in the Shard.

"'It's been a hard few weeks, but the experience has made me a stronger person, and a brush with death is always going to make you appreciate life.'" He smiles.

"Idris and his wife, Michelle, have decided to put the ordeal behind them and forge ahead.

"Asked if he's going to continue with Vipers' Nest, he said, "I'm not quitting now. I want to help entrepreneurs more than ever."

"Turn to page twenty-six for more exclusive photos and insights into Mr and Mrs Beavin.

. . .

"God, he's a shameless arsehole," Fiona said.

Charlotte laughed. "He is." She turned to page twenty-six and started browsing through the photos. "Their apartment is lovely, though. I like those green blinds."

She flicked through the pages, then looked up. "Talking of *Vipers' Nest*, I watched an episode when Helena and I were in the hotel—"

Angus nearly spat out his sip of water.

"I know, I know. There literally wasn't anything else to watch. But actually, the episode I watched was interesting. They all turned down a really good proposal by a designer who makes women's clothes with large pockets."

"That's a great idea. I hate it when my clothes don't have pockets," Fiona commented.

"Iz *really* annoying," Helena agreed.

Charlotte put the magazine down. "Well, I contacted the designer this morning and I'm going to invest in her."

Fiona and Helena congratulated her.

"How much exactly?" Woody asked.

Charlotte tapped the side of her nose. "None of your business, but I did it as an interest-free loan. I don't need the money, of course, but women's pockets are a feminist issue."

"Really?" Euan asked.

"Totally," said Charlotte. "Historically, women's clothes didn't have pockets because their husbands carried their money and possessions. They were supposed to show off their figures at all times, especially when fashion got more figure-hugging."

Fiona nodded. "It's a fine line between being practical and fashionable."

"I've never found it, but now I'm nearing fifty, I'm going for practical."

"And also, if women didn't need bags, then the bag industry would suffer," Fiona replied.

"That's true," Woody stated.

Fiona smiled. "Well, I think it's a great idea. Will you get some samples for me to try?"

"Absolutely. And I can't wait for it to take off and for Idris to wish he'd invested."

Woody laughed. "I hope you're not going to scoop up all his *Vipers' Nest* rejects."

"No, just the ones I think are good ideas."

Angus, who had been sitting and listening, spoke up. "I think you'd be really good on *Vipers' Nest.*"

Charlotte's face softened. "I don't think that's a good idea, but I'll definitely see if there are similar things to invest in."

When the others had gone home, Angus rose and instructed Euan to wait in the car. "I just need a quick word with Charlotte."

He supported her to the office and helped her to a seat. "Is everything all right?" she asked, studying him.

Angus paused, trying to arrange his thoughts. "Yes, but I need to tell you something."

Her eyes widened. "Sounds serious."

"It's nothing bad. In fact, I want you to know that you were brilliant this week."

"I'm always brilliant," Charlotte said, with a smile and a glint in her eye.

"No, I mean it. The way you handled Michelle and

Idris, and I know it wasn't easy. After what they did to you..."

Charlotte shrugged. "It was hard. They mess with my mental health. Then, and now."

"You're so much better than them. Idris is a complete idiot. Not only because he had an affair, but in every other way too."

That made Charlotte laugh. "Are you questioning my judgement in marrying him?"

Angus held up his hands. "No, and you know that's not what I meant."

"Well, despite everything, I have finally moved on from him and I am happy about it. Misty says I dealt with it really well too."

"You did. That must feel good?"

She nodded. "It does."

Angus took a deep breath. Charlotte's fragile post-divorce state had been one of the reasons why he'd never crossed over the line of friendship. Now, that argument had faded away. Charlotte had got herself together.

She sat there, smiling up at him, and Angus felt something more than friendship. He remembered that drunken kiss on the first day they'd met, the feeling of her lips on his. He'd turned her down because she was drunk.

But now— He couldn't think of any reason to stop their friendship developing into something more. They worked together, true, and that could complicate things. But only if they broke up...

"Angus?"

He shook his head as though waking himself from a dream. He needed to give himself some breathing space and examine his feelings. He had to think this through. If he did something out of turn, or in a hurry, it could wreck everything. "Sorry."

"Was that it? You stayed behind because you wanted to inflate my ego?"

He considered, then smiled. "Yes, I did."

She inclined her head. "Thank you. So, are we taking a few days off before our next case?"

"I think that's a very good idea. You've had a difficult time, and I think you need to recharge. Although, to be quite honest, I think you should take a holiday. Isn't there some exotic island you can jet off to?" That would give him time and space to think over his new feelings.

Her brow knitted. "Are you trying to get rid of me?"

"Not at all. I just thought you might like to have some time out, after all you've been through." She looked out of the window. "Maybe I will. But if I do, will you have me back afterwards?"

Angus smiled at her. "Absolutely."

The End

Dear Reader, I hope you enjoyed the third in the series, it would be brilliant if you could leave a review because it helps readers find my books.

IF YOU WANT MORE from Charlotte and Angus, the fourth book is available to order here.

Exe Ray Vision : Lockwood and Darrow Book 4:

Angus and Charlotte are asked to find out who is behind a blackmail attempt at Devon Rugby. But as they draw nearer to who is behind it, they uncover hidden secrets that put them both in danger.

* * *

Dear Reader, I hope you enjoyed the third in the series, it would be brilliant if you could leave a review because it helps readers find my books.

IF YOU WANT MORE from Charlotte and Angus, the fourth book is available here.

Exe Ray Vision : Lockwood and Darrow Book 4:

Angus and Charlotte are asked to find out who is behind a blackmail attempt at Devon Rugby. But as they draw nearer to who is behind it, they uncover hidden secrets that put them both in danger.

* * *

SIGN up to my newsletter on my website to get a FREE Lockwood and Darrow short story.

http://www.suzybussell.com

Suzy xx

Acknowledgments

Many thanks to my amazing and supportive husband and to Liz Hedgecock, my editor and mentor, who also writes mysteries. Check her books out!

About the Author

Suzy started writing at the age of thirty when she penned her first story—a fan fiction—and then graduated on to writing her own characters and tales.

In 2019, she found herself unable to silence the persistent voices of Charlotte and Angus in her thoughts, their vivid characters forcing her hand to starting the 'Lockwood and Darrow' series.

Originally from Hertfordshire, she's called Devon home for two decades. Its picturesque landscapes and unique characters have embedded themselves in almost every story she's penned.

She has a background in computing and a keen interest in technology which naturally weaves its way into her plots to add a touch of modern intrigue. The world of technology has always fascinated her, and merging this with her passion for storytelling felt like a natural progression.

Currently, she lives close to the sea with an amazing and supportive husband, three sons, and two snowshoe cats. When she's not writing, she loves swimming and playing her violin.

Printed in Great Britain
by Amazon

49825820R00101